PURRFECT PASSION

THE MYSTERIES OF MAX 23

NIC SAINT

PURRFECT PASSION

The Mysteries of Max 23

Copyright © 2020 by Nic Saint

Edited by Chereese Graves

www.nicsaint.com

Give feedback on the book at: info@nicsaint.com

facebook.com/nicsaintauthor
@nicsaintauthor

First Edition

Printed in the U.S.A

"**M**ax, can I ask you a question?"

Lazily, I opened my eyes. "Mh?"

"How come we have mice in our basement and next door they don't?"

I shrugged. It was one of those questions no one has an answer to, and certainly not me. "I don't know, Dooley," I said therefore. "Maybe they like our basement better?"

This gave my friend some food for thought, and for a moment I returned to my peaceful slumber. Not for long, though, for Dooley's train of thought was determined to make sure I got no repose whatsoever. His trains of thought are often that way, completely oblivious to my creature comforts.

"So... what is it about Odelia's basement that makes it so appealing to mice?" he asked, launching a follow-up question that compelled me to open my eyes once more and think up a response. I have to tell you, though, it's hard to think when all you want to do is sleep. It had been a particularly eventful night, what with cat choir running overtime, due to the fact that Shanille, cat choir's conductor, had gotten it into her tiny nut that we should take our show on the road, and extend the kind of creative succor we've been providing Hampton Covians to other audiences in other towns, spreading sweetness and light and the caterwauling of a group of tone-deaf cats to all and sundry.

"I have no idea, Dooley," I said. "Maybe we should ask them?"

This idea clearly hadn't yet occurred to my friend, as his face lit up with delight.

"Of course!" he said. "I'll simply go down there and ask them!"

And much to my surprise, he actually up and went!

I frowned as I watched him go. "Um, Dooley?" I said.

He turned, a smile spread across his furry features. "Yes, Max?"

"When I said we should ask them, I didn't mean…"

He gave me that wide-look of his. "Yes, Max?"

"Are you sure this is such a good idea?"

He frowned and a look of confusion wrapped his funny face in frowns. "Of course, Max. It's your idea. And your ideas are always good ideas."

In spite of the fact that his confidence in my cerebral processes warmed the cockles of my heart, I still felt it incumbent upon me to point out a fatal flaw in this, my own, plan. "We've talked about this, remember? When we made our peace with Hector and Helga we agreed that the basement was theirs, and the rest of the house ours."

He gave me a look of bewilderment. "I don't understand."

"The basement has officially been turned into a no-go zone for cats," I explained. "It's their territory now, and we're not supposed to tread there if we can help it."

"But… this is our house, Max. We have a right to go where we want, don't we?"

"Well, not anymore. Under the terms of the peace treaty

we arranged with the mice, this house has now been divided into two separate zones. There is a cat zone..." With an all-encompassing sweep of my paw I motioned to the living room, the kitchen and the upstairs. "And there's the mice zone—in other words, the basement."

His bewilderment was absolute. "But... are you sure this is legal?"

I suppressed the urge to roll my eyes. "If you mean was there a notary present when we came to this agreement, then no, there wasn't. But it was either that or have them traipse all over the house, raid our fridge, steal the kibble from our bowls whenever they felt like it, and turn our lives into a living hell. It's an arrangement for our mutual benefit. The mice can live their lives unencumbered, raising a family of healthy, happy little pinkies and pups, and we can relax and save face in front of Odelia and Chase."

It had taken a lot of persuading on my part to get my human on board. Odelia shares most humans' visceral aversion to all things rodent, and the mere suggestion that we'd give these critters and their offspring a permanent home in her home (and our home) seemed repugnant to her. But I simply appealed to her softer side and even she had to admit it was an arrangement that offered a lot of benefits. As long as these mice occupied the basement, no other mice would move in. Better the mice you know than the mice you don't, if you see what I mean. And when I personally introduced her to Hector, and translated the little fella's words for her, and told her they had come in peace and had promised us to keep the basement absolutely free of droppings, she relented, and so did her boyfriend Chase.

Though the latter contrived a look of bewilderment very similar to Dooley's. He probably hadn't expected when he started dating Odelia that at some point in the near future he'd find himself negotiating with a colony of mice, a cat officiating the peace treaty.

"I still don't see why the basement should be off-limits," said Dooley. "It's still our house, and they're just guests."

"Look at it this way, Dooley," I said, deciding to try a different tack. "It's as if you're a property owner. And the mice are your tenants."

"Tenants who don't pay rent."

"True, true," I admitted. "The point I'm trying to make, though, is that a landlord can't simply walk into a tenant's house or apartment, see?"

"He can't?" asked Dooley, much surprised by this strange legal quirk.

"No, he cannot. There are laws protecting a tenant's privacy, and a landlord can't simply barge in whenever he likes. He has to get the tenant's permission first."

"So I have to get Hector's permission before I can set paw in the basement?"

"Pretty much," I agreed.

"And what about Odelia? Does she have to get Hector's permission, too?"

"Um, no, I guess she doesn't. The arrangement is between cats and mice only."

His face cleared. "Great! Then I'll simply ask Odelia to ask Hector why they like it here so much. And I'll tag along as Odelia's official translator, just like a delegation of Swaziland would bring along their translator when attending the United Nations General Assembly." And with these words he trotted off in the direction of the staircase, presumably to rouse Odelia from sleep so she could pose this all-important question.

This time I did roll my eyes, then lay down my head on the sofa cushion I'd singled out for my own, and went back to sleep. The plight of the rodent family that had moved into the basement might fascinate and intrigue my friend, but it certainly did not fascinate me. You may say I'm a lousy cat for allowing mice to move into my domain, and I'd tell you that my peace of mind is worth a lot more to me than any slings and arrows you can aim at me. That and my daily dose of kibble, of course.

And I'd just fallen into a peaceful slumber once more when the sound of a flapping pet flap told me that the prospect of a nice nap was not in my near future just yet. When I opened my eyes I found myself gazing into the familiar face of Brutus, and he wasn't looking very happy at all. His next words confirmed my assessment of his mental state.

"Max, you have to help me. It's Harriet. She's gone completely mad!"

*T*o be absolutely honest with you, Brutus's announcement didn't surprise me. I'd already had the feeling that Harriet was brooding on something. Even her customary solo performance during cat choir had had a different quality last night, as she'd seemed distracted and a little surly, and had dropped even more notes than usual. Even Shanille had felt compelled to ask the prissy Persian if everything was all right, receiving a typical snappish response for her trouble.

"What is it this time?" I asked therefore, starting to feel as if this nap I'd been anticipating with such eagerness was starting to look like a lost cause.

"She wants to put our relationship to the test by joining a reality show," said Brutus.

I frowned. "I'm sorry, Brutus, but you're going to have to run that by me again. I didn't quite catch your drift."

He was too wired to take a seat, and had resorted to pacing the rug, going so far as to extend his nails and plucking little tufts of fiber from Odelia's nice carpet. It just goes to show the extent of his exasperation. It's one of the reasons why I've remained a bachelor until now: my closest friends are frankly the best advertisement for bachelorhood.

"She's been watching this reality show with Gran lately. Passion Island? Gran is hooked on the thing, and so is Harriet. It's all they talk about. And now Harriet has decided she wants in. She figures it's the best way to see if we're really meant to be together."

"But... I didn't even know she had doubts about that."

"Me neither! But watching Passion Island has made her think."

"Uh-oh," I muttered.

"And she's been pushing Gran to get her on the show, and it looks like Gran thinks this might not be such a bad idea, only cats aren't allowed anywhere near the island."

"For a good reason," I said, nodding. No reality show fans want to be distracted by the sight of a couple of cats slinking into the frame and obscuring their view.

"Yeah, but Gran says she can probably make the producers change their minds. Or maybe even get them to create a spin-off. Cat Passion Island. She figures it would give people the best of both worlds: adorable cats doing what cats do best, and a healthy dose of drama."

"But... no viewer would understand what the cats are saying," I pointed out. "And where would be the fun in that?"

"Exactly what I said!" said Brutus, becoming more and more agitated. "But do you think they'll listen to the voice of reason? Oh, no."

"I'm sure nothing will come of it," I tried to reassure the butch black cat. "You know what Gran is like. She always has some bee buzzing in her bonnet, but rarely has the where-withal to see her wild ideas through to fruition."

He gave me a look of hope. "You think so? You've known Gran longer than I have."

"Trust me," I said. "This idea will simply fizzle out and die before you can say kibble."

"Kibble," said Brutus earnestly, and plunked himself down, slightly mollified. And I could see his point. Gran may have the attention span of a goldfish, but Harriet is one of those cats that don't stop until they get what they want. If she had her mind set on being in some goofy reality show, she'd keep harping on the theme until she got her wish.

I decided not to share this little insight into Harriet's psyche with the latter's mate, though, as I was still holding out a tiny hope I'd get the chance to have that sweet nap.

And as Brutus mulled over my words, I shifted in my seat and accidentally hit a button on the remote control, inadvertently turning on the TV. And while I was wondering why the TV had suddenly started pouring out its usual dose of frenetic programming on an unsuspecting world, Brutus sprang to his paws again, vibrating with excitement, his nose pointing in the direction of the darned thing like a pointing dog.

"That's it!" he cried. "That's the show that's ruining my life!"

I directed a curious eye at the goggle box and saw that a small group of young women was seated around a fire, all staring intently at a tablet computer, held up by a platinum-haired and sophisticated-looking woman. On the tablet's screen, grainy footage of a man and a woman lying in bed together appeared, and suddenly one of the women brought her hands to her face and started sobbing uncontrollably.

"Prepare yourself for a shock, Sookie," said the sophisticated woman, who appeared to be the show's host. "The next images will be tough for you to watch."

We were regaled with images of the same couple in bed, only this time all that was visible was a shapeless form underneath the sheets, and those very same sheets were moving in a very suspicious way indeed. It was obvious the couple were in the throes of a passionate spate of lovemaking, bumping and grinding with careless abandon.

The woman named Sookie, the one who'd been sobbing, now wailed like a banshee. "Not my Bennie-ie-ie-ie!" she cried.

"Yes, I'm afraid your Bennie has succumbed to the wily ways of seductress Mia," said the show host, barely suppressing a hint of satisfaction.

"Oh, my God," said Brutus, looking on with fascination. "I never thought Bennie would cheat on Sookie. They were the perfect couple! Everybody said so!"

It was obvious to me that Brutus was as big a fan of this Passion Island bonanza as Harriet and Gran.

Just then, Dooley came trudging down the stairs again, a very sleepy-looking Odelia in tow. "So what's all this about the United Nations General Assembly?" she asked.

But Dooley had become distracted by the footage on TV. He stared at the wild sheet tussle for a moment, then asked, "What are those people doing, Max?"

Brutus and I immediately scrambled to grab the remote and change the channel. Unfortunately in our efforts to do so, the thing dropped to the floor and skipped underneath the couch. And as I aimlessly reached for the gizmo, I saw how Dooley approached the screen and stared at the footage of Sookie's Bennie-ie-ie-ie and wily seductress Mia, whoever she was, performing feats of acrobatics, their modesty only covered by a thin sheet.

"Are they playing a game?" asked Dooley, wide-eyed now as he took in the scene.

"Um, yeah," I said, still fruitlessly reaching underneath the couch. "Yeah, they're playing a game of hide and seek."

"Looks like they found each other," said Dooley, quite astutely I might add.

"Oh, is that Passion Island?" asked Odelia, stifling a yawn. "I love that show."

Brutus emitted a low groan. "*Everybody* loves that show," he said.

"Yeah, even Mom and Dad watch every episode." She frowned at the screen. "This is a rerun though, right?" Like a true addict, she sounded worried she'd missed something.

"Yeah, they're gearing up for a new season, and started airing last season's episodes to whet people's appetites," said Brutus, as the expert he clearly was.

Dooley had turned his head sideways and was still watching the couple intently. "It looks like they're rubbing against each other," he said finally, still that puzzled look on his face. "Why are they rubbing against each other, Max?"

"Um, I guess one of them has an itch," I said, eliciting a smile from Odelia. Then, finally getting hip to my predicament, she fished the remote from underneath the couch, and quickly changed channels. A weatherman started waxing poetic about a low-pressure system moving in from the East, or it could have been the West, and I breathed a sigh of relief. The danger had been averted, and Dooley's innocence was safe once more.

"Harriet wants to be on that show," said Brutus. "And Gran told her she's going to help her."

Odelia laughed. "Of course she did." She patted Brutus on the head. "Don't you worry about a thing, Brutus. The day Harriet is selected for Passion Island is the day hell freezes over." And with these sage words, she entered the kitchen to start fixing herself and Chase some breakfast.

Suddenly the sliding glass door that looks out onto the backyard opened and Gran walked in, followed by none other than Harriet herself. They both had those looks of determination in their eyes that spelled trouble.

"Odelia, there's something I need to talk to you about," said Gran in a tone of voice that brooked no contest.

"Oh, hey, Gran," said Odelia. "Are you joining us for breakfast?"

"Yeah, sure," said Gran. "Look, I'm going crazy next door, with your mom and dad in Europe, and I was thinking—"

"Coffee?"

"Yeah. So I've been thinking—"

"Milk and sugar?"

"You know I take my coffee black, honey," said Gran, taking a seat on one of the high stools at the kitchen counter.

Odelia smiled, and I could tell she wasn't fully awake yet. It takes a heavy dose of caffeine to accomplish that minor feat, and she hadn't had hers yet.

Chase came stomping down the stairs, yawning cavernously and stretching. "I had the weirdest dream," he announced to no one in particular. "I dreamt that I was on an island and there were only women. Can you imagine? I was the only male on an island filled with the most gorgeous wo —" He suddenly became aware he was being intently watched by his future grandmother-in-law, and quickly shut up. Waking up on an island filled with gorgeous women may be every man's fantasy, it clearly wasn't Gran's.

Odelia took it in stride, though. "Well, isn't that a coincidence? I dreamt I was on a desert island filled with gorgeous men, all catering to my every need. Crazy, huh?"

Immediately, Chase's expression soured. "I don't know what's so wonderful about an island full of men," he grumbled as he dug into the fridge and came out with the OJ.

"Well, I enjoyed it," said Odelia. "You were saying, Gran?"

"Thank you," said Gran. "Before I was so rudely *interrupted...*" She raised her voice as she spoke this last word, casting a censorious look at Chase, which the latter ignored as he was clearly still ruminating on Odelia's island-of-gorgeous-males dream. "... I was going to tell you that I've decided to move in with you guys again. Isn't that great?"

Chase, who'd been glugging down his orange juice straight from the container, choked and spat out a stream of the orange stuff straight into the sink. Some of it came out of his nose.

"You what?" he said, not exactly with the kind of warmth and welcoming attitude a woman expects from the man who's about to plight his troth to her granddaughter.

"It's just that I've been feeling a little lonely lately, all alone in that big old house."

"You have your cats," Chase pointed out as he wiped his face with a paper towel.

"It's not the same without my daughter and her husband," said Gran decidedly, "so I've decided to move in with you until they're back from their trip through Europe. Now if you could prepare me a slice of toast, very crisp, lightly buttered, there's a good boy."

I saw how Chase exchanged a flabbergasted look with Odelia, the latter merely responding with a sigh and a shrug, and I felt for the big guy. I mean, it's one thing to fall in love with a chirpy, happy, peppy blonde and move in with her, but quite another to get a slightly irritating older lady as a surprise bonus when you do.

"If gran is moving in with Odelia and Chase," said Harriet, "Brutus and I are also moving back in."

"Back?" I asked. "What do you mean, back? You've only ever lived next door, Harriet."

"Yeah, and now I'm moving in with you, Max," she said tersely. "Got a problem with that?"

Warning bells went off in my head, and a good thing they did, as many a cat has been on the receiving end of Harriet's sharp tongue, and claws, in the past, and I wasn't in the mood for either a tongue lashing, or a demonstration of just how sharp those claws were.

"No, no," I hurried to say. "It's perfectly fine with me."

"If you do move in," said Dooley, "we'll probably have to negotiate a new peace treaty. Just like we did with Hector and Helga. I suggest Max and I get the downstairs, and you guys can have the upstairs. The basement, of course, belongs to the mice."

"What are you talking about, Dooley?" asked Harriet, an expression of annoyance having crept up her pretty face.

"Well, when Hector moved in, Max negotiated a peace treaty," Dooley explained, as I made frantic gestures for him to stop talking. Gestures, unfortunately, he blithely ignored. "So it's only fair we do the same thing with you. Max, do you want to start?" He gave Harriet a warm smile. "Max is a skilled negotiator. Isn't that right, Max?"

I cleared my throat as Harriet turned those fiery eyes on me. "Is that a fact?" she said.

"Well, obviously there's a slight difference between a colony of mice moving in and two dear, dear friends like yourself and Brutus," I prevaricated.

"Oh, is there now?" said Harriet, having adopted the kind of smooth tone that usually precipitates an outburst of volcanic proportions.

"Yeah, so I don't think we need to go through all of that nonsense. Instead I'd like to extend the paw of friendship and bid you welcome in our humble home. *Mi casa es su casa*, and all that."

Harriet, whose lips had drawn together in a thin line, nodded once. "Sometimes, Max, I wonder if you really are as smart as you think you are. First off, this isn't *your* casa at all. This is *our* casa, and so for you to welcome me into my own home is simply… simply…" She stomped her foot. "Aaargh!" she finished her statement with some eloquence, and made a beeline for the kitchen and her bowl of kibble.

"We probably should tell Odelia to place Harriet and Brutus's bowls on the landing," said Dooley with a thoughtful glance at Harriet's retreating back. "And your litter boxes, of course," he added for Brutus's benefit.

I had a feeling that it was going to take me the better part of my designated nap time to try and explain to Dooley that there was going to be no peace treaty and no divvying up the house. But then what else is new?

4

Odelia and Chase were enjoying a hearty breakfast with Odelia's grandmother while the cats made arrangements for Harriet and Brutus to move in—though technically cats never 'move in' anywhere. They make their home wherever they like, and their humans simply have to accept it.

"So you miss Tex, huh?" said Chase as he ladled up his power breakfast. It consisted of oats, fruits, a fermented almond paste he made himself, and dates to add sweetness.

Gran's eyes shot daggers at Odelia's fiancé. "Of course I don't miss Tex. It's just that at my age any change of routine is a lot harder to bear. You'll see when you're as old as me."

"You're not that old, Gran," said Odelia, earning herself a smile from her grandmother.

"Thanks, honey," said Gran, affectionately patting her granddaughter on the cheek. She brought her piece of toast, now liberally smeared with strawberry jam, to her lips and took a big bite. There was nothing wrong with Gran's appetite.

"I miss Mom and Dad," said Odelia. "Though I'm happy they finally got the chance to fulfill an old dream."

Her mother and father had left the week before for a three-week trip around Europe. London, Paris, Rome, Venice, Amsterdam... They were doing it all and doing it in style. Odelia had been getting tons of pictures, and her mother's Facebook feed was full of snapshots of the two of them in front of Buckingham Palace, the Eiffel Tower, the Colosseum... And in every picture they looked a little tanner and more relaxed.

"I wouldn't mind going on a trip around Europe myself," said Gran now. "Though it wouldn't be much fun on my own. I'd have to find a friend to tag along."

She darted a meaningful glance at Odelia, but the latter held up her hand. "I can't get away right now. I have a big story to tackle for Dan, and he'd kill me if I took off." Not to mention that her piggy bank couldn't afford the financial onslaught of three weeks in Europe.

"How about Scarlett?" asked Chase. "I thought you and her were BFFs now?"

Gran's face sagged. "It's one thing to finally be reconciled again, but another to be joined at the hip for almost a month while you hopscotch around an entire continent."

"I'm glad you two are getting along so well again," said Odelia. "And maybe you could start by going on a weekend trip together? See how it goes?"

Gran didn't look convinced. "Mh," she responded unenthusiastically. "She friended me on Facebook the other day, and has been sending me a never-ending string of personal messages."

"That's very nice of her," said Odelia encouragingly. "It shows she really wants this friendship to work."

"All pictures of half-naked men," Gran clarified. "I'm starting to think the woman is some kind of nymphomaniac.

I mean, I like the male form just as much as the next gal, but there are limits to the number of oiled-up pecs and glistening six-packs you can see."

"She probably thought you'd like it."

"Yeah, well, I don't, and when I see her I'll tell her in no uncertain terms what I think of all of this spam." And with these words, she got down from her stool, dumped her plate in the sink and stalked off, presumably to start her move into the spare room.

"She's in a mood," Chase remarked.

"I think she misses Mom and Dad a lot more than she's letting on," said Odelia. "I miss them, and I don't even live with them."

"Looks like we're turning our office-slash-gym into a spare bedroom again, huh?"

"Yeah, looks like it," said Odelia, and placed a hand on her understanding boyfriend's arm. "Sorry about that."

"No, it's fine," said Chase. "I like your grandmother. She can be a handful, but she has a good heart, and I'm more than happy to accommodate her for two—"

"Three."

Chase grimaced. "Three weeks."

Odelia smiled. The last time Gran had moved in things had gotten a little tense. She hoped that this time the old lady would behave.

Her phone produced its telltale series of beeps, announcing a message from Mom, and she swiped to open the message. She smiled when she found herself glancing at her parents standing in front of what looked like a Roman centurion, goofy smiles on their faces, as Dad pretended to be engaged in a display of sword fight with the Roman.

Chase, glancing over her shoulder, said, "I can understand your gran. I wouldn't mind taking a little vacation myself.

Things have been pretty hectic at the office lately, and I'm due a vacation."

"Yeah, me, too," Odelia intimated. "Not Europe, though. We don't have the time or the budget."

"How about a weekend trip to the Keys? I think we could afford that, right?"

"Let's talk about it once Mom and Dad are back," Odelia suggested. A weekend trip was fine, but what she really longed for, she now realized, was the kind of vacation that involved a lot of lazing around on a tropical beach somewhere, the blue azure water lapping at her feet, waiters at her every beck and call, umbrella drink in hand and a good book. But since that wasn't in the cards, she simply sighed and put down her phone.

Just then, the doorbell chimed, and she got up, wondering who it could be. She wasn't expecting any visitors. She opened the door to find her uncle standing on the mat, accompanied by a woman she'd never seen before.

Uncle Alec smiled widely, and said, "Would you like to go to Thailand for three weeks?"

5

I pricked up my ears at the mention of the word 'Thailand'. As everyone knows, cats aren't frequent travelers, but lately we'd already flown to LA and even the UK, all in the wake of our human, who's something of an amateur sleuth when the mood strikes.

Dooley and I locked eyes, and I could see that he, too, was impressed by this sudden turn of events.

"Thailand," said Brutus. "Isn't that where they eat cats and dogs for dinner?"

"Brutus!" Harriet cried.

"I'm sure they don't eat cats in Thailand," I said reassuringly.

"No, they do," Brutus insisted. "And dogs."

We all watched Uncle Alec step inside, followed by a young woman of petite dimensions. She had long dark hair and horn-rimmed glasses perched on a cute little nub of a nose. She glanced around nervously, not entirely at ease. I wondered if she was the travel agent Uncle Alec had secured for this unexpected trip he'd just mentioned.

"I don't want to go to Thailand, Max," said Dooley, wasting no time getting worked up. "I don't like to be eaten."

"Nobody likes to be eaten, Dooley," I assured him.

"What's this all about?" asked Chase, throwing down his napkin and joining his commanding officer in the living room.

"First let me introduce this young lady," said Uncle Alec. "Kimmy Flannery, meet my niece Odelia and her future husband Chase, also known as Detective Kingsley. Kimmy works for a production company in the capacity of assistant producer, isn't that right, Kimmy?"

Kimmy nodded. "I work for Sunshine Pictures. I don't know if you've heard of them?"

Both Odelia and Chase shook their heads.

"No, I guess the product we make is more famous than the company. Passion Island is our main product right now, and has been a big hit for the past five seasons, now in prep for season six."

Odelia's mouth opened, and Chase's jaw dropped. And when I glanced around, I could see that both Brutus and Harriet were very impressed indeed as well.

"This is serendipity," Harriet said in a low voice. "I'm a believer, you guys."

"A believer in what?" asked Dooley.

"Serendipity!" said Harriet.

"I've heard about that," said Dooley. "It's a national park in Africa."

"I think that's the Serengeti," I said, and brought my paw to my lips in the universal sign of 'Better shut up now or risk Harriet's ire.'

"First off, this is not official," said Kimmy, as everyone distributed themselves amongst the couches, or at least those spots that hadn't been taken up by yours truly and my three friends. Cats are not easy to dislodge, so we simply stayed put, even if it meant that Uncle Alec had to remain standing, and Chase had to take the arm of the couch.

"I've worked for Sunshine Pictures from its inception," said Kimmy, as she glanced around nervously, as if expecting nefarious elements to spring up from behind the curtains. "And don't get me wrong: I love my job, and my colleagues. But something very strange has been happening, and I don't know what to do about it, or how to proceed."

"Kimmy is Charlene's niece," Uncle Alec explained. "And when Charlene heard about what happened, she told her to come and see me."

"At first I didn't want to," said Kimmy, giving Uncle Alec an apologetic look. "In fact going to the police was the last thing I wanted to do."

"But Charlene told her not to look upon me as a cop," said Uncle Alec. "I mean, I'm a cop, of course, but I'm also a guy who has a very talented niece—a niece who's a natural sleuth." He gave Odelia a wink.

"So what's the problem?" asked Chase. "What's going on?"

Kimmy took a deep breath and launched into her story. "I'm not sure, but for the past five years we've staged five productions of Passion Island, with increasing success. And in those same five years, five of our participants have gone missing."

"Probably eaten alive," Brutus muttered.

"What do you mean?" asked Odelia with a frown.

"I don't know if you're familiar with our show?" asked Kimmy.

"I am," said Odelia.

"Then I don't have to explain that four men and four women participate each season. It's my job to make sure they're taken care of, not only their physical well-being but also psychologically. Which is why we always stay in touch with all participants even after the show has been taped and aired. Well, the strange thing is that I haven't been able to contact several of the women of the past seasons, five altogether, one from each show."

"You mean the winners?"

"Not the winners," said Kimmy. "Contestants, not seductresses."

"What's a seductress, Max?" asked Dooley.

"Um…" I said.

"In Passion Island four couples are sent to Thailand," Harriet explained. "The men are dropped on one island, the women on another. Once there, the men are joined by six seductresses and the women by six seducers, whose sole task it is to, well, seduce them. Make them perform an act of infidelity. If the candidates succumb to the charms, they lose. The couple that manages to remain faithful to each other wins the big prize."

"What a weird show," I said. I hadn't really paid attention to Passion Island, as I'm not all that big on reality shows—they rarely feature cats, after all, or kibble—but this concept struck me as a little—or a lot—cruel.

"So what do you think happened to these women?" asked Chase.

"I don't know. All I know is that I can't seem to reach them."

"Have you talked to their families? Maybe they simply don't want to have anything to do with the show anymore," Odelia suggested.

"Oh, I've tried everything. And it's not as if they've actually been reported missing. In every single case they've decided to sever all contact with their loved ones."

"But why?"

"Well, four women said they'd found Mr. Right, and got married after a whirlwind romance—so whirlwind they didn't even invite their family or friends to the nuptials. And in one case the woman said she'd joined a convent in the Himalayas."

"So... not exactly missing," said Chase.

"None of these women has skyped or been seen alive since their alleged marriages or entry into monastic life. They've sent the occasional text or email, but no pictures or any other contact. No phone calls, no nothing, and their families are justifiably worried."

"So why don't they go to the police?" asked Odelia.

"Because they've been specifically asked not to. Allegedly by the women themselves."

"And you think something else is going on."

"Yes, I do. I think all five of them have been abducted, and a cover story has been fed to their families. Only there's nothing I can prove, and the families don't want the police to get involved."

"They believe the cover story."

Kimmy nodded. "They're afraid that if they talk to the police they might never see their loved ones again."

"It's a pretty strange story," said Chase, rubbing his chin.

"I know, and I didn't know what to do, until I happened to mention it to my aunt, and she referred me to Alec, who referred me to you." She directed a desperate look at Odelia. "I have a gut feeling something bad has happened to these women, and I don't know where else to turn."

ollowing Odelia's instructions, Vesta had found the spare mattress in the attic. Chase was supposed to get it down for her, but apparently he'd been detained. And since Vesta had never been the type of person to sit and wait, she'd decided to get the darn thing down herself.

Which in her case meant she'd simply shoved the mattress over to the attic door by giving it a couple of good kicks, and then, like a seasoned football player, had punted it down the stairs, sending it tumbling into the abyss.

The mattress landed on its feet—or in this case, since mattresses rarely have feet, on its side—and it only took another couple of good shoves and kicks to get it into position, squeezed in between Chase's dumbbell rack, his home trainer, and Odelia's desk.

"What a dumbbell," Vesta mumbled under her breath. Why people bothered with fitness she'd never understand. If God had wanted humans to work out, he'd have outfitted them with leg warmers, a sweatband and a glittery leotard, like Jane Fonda.

She glanced around. It wasn't exactly the coziest place in the world, but for now it would do. She didn't like to admit it, but she hated waking up in an empty house, and going to bed without the comforting sounds of Tex and Marge brushing their teeth and hitting the hay same time as her.

She was getting pretty soft and mushy in her old age, but that couldn't be helped. Like her cats, she was a creature both of comfort and habit, and if Marge and Tex decided to desert her, at least she had her granddaughter and that goofy cop she insisted on dating to tide her over until the European traveling couple's triumphant return.

And she was trudging down the stairs, reminding herself she needed to ask Chase to switch the TV to her favorite channel and keep it there for the duration, when she heard the two words in the English language that never failed to give her a jolt of pleasant anticipation and excitement: Passion Island.

"So you'll do it?" an unfamiliar woman's voice was asking.

"I'll have to ask my boss, but if he says yes, we'll do it," said Odelia. "The only problem is: I can't really afford to spend three weeks in Thailand on my salary."

"That's all right. I've arranged for you and Detective Kingsley to join the show as one of the four couples."

Vesta, as she entered the living room, slightly out of breath, both from excitement and the fact that she'd practically skipped the final step in her eagerness to join the conversation and had had to perform a number of complicated and acrobatic movements in order to stay upright, said, "Me too! I'm going as a couple, too!"

"Gran!" said Odelia, surprised to see her aged relative burst onto the scene like a cuckoo from a clock. She smiled at a young thin woman with glasses, and said, "This is my grandmother. She's a big fan of Passion Island."

"Where do I sign up?" said Vesta, licking her lips and rubbing her hands.

"Um…" said the woman, giving Vesta a decidedly skeptical once-over.

She directed an anxious glance at Odelia, who said, reassuringly, "Gran is fine. She won't tell anyone what she just heard. Isn't that right, Gran?"

"Who cares? I want to be on the show!"

"I'm afraid…" the woman began.

"Oh, no!" Vesta lamented plaintively. "Don't tell me you're not going to take me with you to Thailand! I want to go! I want to be on the show!"

"It's a miracle Kimmy has been able to get Odelia and Chase on the show," said Alec. "You can't expect her to get you signed up, too, Ma."

"But—"

"You don't even have a partner."

"But—"

"No," said Alec, using his cop voice. "And no means no."

"But, but, but…"

"Listen, I'll send you a link that gives you exclusive behind-the-scenes access," said the woman named Kimmy. "How does that sound?"

"Lousy! I'm going to Thailand with you! Odelia?" She turned to her granddaughter, and gave her her best puppy-dog look. "Pretty please?"

But her granddaughter was as unyielding as Kimmy. "I'm sorry, Gran," she said. "Not this time."

She set her jaw, gave the collected company a mulish look, and said, "This isn't over!" then turned on her heel and strode off.

If Odelia and that Kimmy person really thought they'd deny her the opportunity to join her favorite show ever, they had another thing coming. And as she stomped out into the backyard, through the hole in the hedge and into her own backyard, the first contours of a plan started to form in her mind.

Whether Odelia liked it or not, she was going to Thailand. "Just you wait and see," she muttered, as she slammed the kitchen door and took out her phone. She knew just who to call.

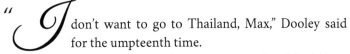

"I don't want to go to Thailand, Max," Dooley said for the umpteenth time.

"And we're not," I responded, reiterating what I'd told him all those previous times.

We were walking down the street on our customary foray into town, eager to extract some snippets of news from our usual correspondents in our fair town. Snippets we faithfully relay to Odelia, who collects the greatest hits and puts them in her newspaper.

"But Odelia is going, and Chase, and there's no way they'll go without dragging us along," Dooley said, and not unreasonably so.

"First off, it's not even a sure thing Odelia is going," I said.

"But she promised Kimmy she'd go and look for those missing women."

"She said she was going to ask her boss. That's a different thing altogether. And if I know Dan, he'll probably say no. Odelia has a full plate right now, and there's no way he'll allow her to disappear for three weeks. Also, didn't you hear what Chase said this morning? He has a lot of work at the police precinct, so he's not going, either. And if they're not going, we're not going."

"I hope so," said Dooley. He didn't look convinced, nor did I blame him. When the call of adventure sounds, Odelia is often all too eager to heed it, and usually she likes to take us along with her, as her eyes and ears in the world of pets and other furry creatures. Only I was with Dooley on this one. The prospect of becoming a yummy snack for the discerning Thai didn't hold a lot of appeal for me. I like to eat, but that doesn't mean I also like to be eaten, if you see what I mean.

We'd arrived in the heart of town, and made a beeline for our friend and frequent collaborator Kingman, Hampton Cove's unofficial feline mayor. He was lounging on the side-walk, regaling a small gathering of—strictly female—felines with his tall tales.

"Hey, you guys," he said by way of greeting once we hove into view. "So there I was," he continued fascinating the six or so adoring females, "hanging from a single claw, and it was only through the sheer strength of my not inconsiderable muscular prowess that I managed to hoist myself up and back to safety. Meanwhile the rat, which was easy twice my size, was first stunned then turned vicious. And as it yelled, 'Why don't you just dieeeeeeee!' and came charging in my direction, pure hatred written all over its hideous features, fangs dripping with saliva, ready to pounce and shove me into the abyss, I—"

"I saw that movie!" Dooley suddenly interrupted. "I don't remember what it was called…"

"Please be quiet," said Kingman. "So the rat came storming in my direction and I decided to take a stand. 'You will not pass!' I called out to the vicious creature."

"Ooh, Kingman!" one of the females cooed. "You're such a hero!"

"We saw it together," said Dooley, once again interrupting Kingman's narrative. "It was playing on Wilbur's little TV." He gestured to the small TV set Wilbur Vickery, Kingman's human, likes to keep next to the cash register, so he can watch sports when business is slow. Though he often watches when business isn't slow, too, it must be said.

"Shush, Dooley," said Kingman. "Can't you see I'm in the middle of something? So that rat came zooming in my direction, claws out, eyes red and bulging and—"

"And then the rat attacked and they fought and by some miracle that brave little cat won the fight and flung the rat into the ravine. I liked it. The lead cat was quite the actor."

"Dooley!" Kingman cried, as his feline audience began to show signs of restlessness.

"Yes, Kingman?" said Dooley.

But too late. The fatal fascination Kingman had held over his admirers was broken, and as they dispersed, aiming such choice words at Kingman as 'fake' and 'show-off', Kingman shouted back, "But the story isn't finished! Ladies, please!"

But no dice. Kingman had been booed off the stage and his fans were fans no more.

He heaved a deep sigh. "So hard these days to educate and entertain. One faux pas and they're gone." He directed a not-too-friendly glance at my friend. "And your babbling didn't help. Why did you have to go and interrupt me just when I was going so well?"

"Odelia is thinking about sending us to Thailand to be eaten," said Dooley. "And we need your advice, Kingman. I don't want to be eaten, and neither does Max."

Kingman's wrath quickly dissipated. "Thailand? Eaten?"

"How many times to I have to tell you, Dooley?" I said. "We're not going to Thailand. And even if we were, I'm sure Odelia wouldn't allow people to eat us."

"Odelia is going to Thailand?" asked Kingman, interested. "On vacation?"

"Not a vacation," I said. "Five women who participated in a reality show have disappeared, and the show's assistant producer has asked Odelia to investigate."

"What reality show?"

"Passion Island."

"I love that show!" Kingman cried. "Wilbur watches it all the time. He even signed up for the auditions but he wasn't selected."

"Auditions?" I asked. "But I thought Wilbur was a bachelor?"

"Yeah, shouldn't he audition for The Bachelor instead?" asked Dooley, indicating he knew his reality shows well. Then again, Dooley spends a lot of time with Gran, and if anyone is a reality show aficionado, it's Odelia's grandmother.

"He wanted to try out for seducer," Kingman explained.

We all glanced up at Wilbur. The gaunt, white-bearded, rheumy-eyed old man was watching Tom & Jerry and chuckling delightedly, slapping his thighs in the process.

"He doesn't look like a seducer," Dooley said, and I thought that was probably the understatement of the year.

"No, the producers didn't even invite him," said Kingman. "Too bad. Wilbur said he could have done a lot of damage."

I winced at the notion of Wilbur Vickery putting on his best seduction game. Somehow the prospect didn't hold a lot of appeal.

"Look, if Odelia decides to go to Thailand, all you gotta do is say no," said Kingman. "She's your human, but that doesn't mean you have to do what she says. You simply tell her no, not this time, and you stay home. Someone will be there to look after you guys, right?"

"Yeah, Gran definitely isn't going," I said.

"See? Problem solved. In fact maybe it will do you some good. No Odelia means no cases to solve or clues to hunt. Consider this a nice little vacation."

Dooley's face cleared, and I have to confess that the prospect of spending three weeks doing absolutely nothing sounded pretty sweet to me, too. Eating, sleeping... more eating.

Three cats came sashaying down the sidewalk, wagging their tails, and Kingman gave them his best grin. "Hey, ladies, did I tell you the story of the big hairy rat and how I defeated that sucker?"

It was clear we'd just been dismissed, and so we went on our way.

"Kingman is right, Max," said Dooley. "If Odelia goes to Thailand we simply tell her we don't want to go, on account of the fact that we don't like to be eaten. She'll understand."

I agreed wholeheartedly. And so it was with a spring in our step and the prospect of three weeks vacation on our minds that we continued our daily perambulation of Hampton Cove.

8

*O*delia was in her editor's office, discussing Kimmy's request. Dan, his brow creased and his long white beard waggling, was clearly thinking hard.

"So… you'd have to go all the way to Thailand for three weeks?"

"Kimmy can get both me and Chase signed up as one of the four couples. It would be perfect. We could talk to everyone involved in the show's production and find out what's going on."

"It could be dangerous," Dan said.

"I know, but Chase will be there in case something goes wrong."

"Mh…" said Dan, clearly not fully convinced. He was fingering his beard now, presumably digging around for crumbs he'd missed during his morning grooming session. Odelia had always wondered how men like Dan managed to keep their beards so immaculate. If she had a beard like that it would very quickly turn into a receptacle for anything that failed to go down the hatch while indulging in the occasional snack or sitting down for her three square meals a day.

"You don't think it's a good idea?"

"Mh…" Dan repeated, and swiveled a little in his swivel chair. "I took a quick look at the women Kimmy claims have gone missing, and it strikes me that they're all the same type: blond, slim and pretty." He waggled his bushy brows. "Just like someone else I know."

"Oh? Who?"

"You, of course! You're the spitting image of the five women who've disappeared. So if there's some kidnapper at work who likes to snatch women who've been on Passion Island he'll grab you in a heartbeat."

Odelia laughed. "No one in his right mind would try to snatch me, Dan."

His response was another brow waggle.

"I'm not even pretty!"

"Oh, you foolish woman," said Dan with a sigh. "Of course you are. And you have to wonder if you're not putting yourself in harm's way here, simply because Kimmy doesn't want to hire a professional."

"I am a professional," said Odelia, expanding a little.

Dan gave her a warm smile. "A professional reporter, not a professional detective."

"It would make for a great story," she said, deciding to dangle the carrot. She knew Dan was a sucker for a killer story, whether it was related to Hampton Cove or not.

"It is a great story," he agreed. "At least if the reporter writing it survives long enough to hand in her copy."

"Nothing's gonna happen to me, Dan," she assured her boss. "Like I said, Chase will be there, and so will my cats."

"Your cats won't be able to stop anyone from grabbing you, and if I understand the concept of Passion Island, and I think I do, Chase will be dumped on a different island and not allowed anywhere near you. They'll even take away your phone."

"It'll be fine," she said with a careless wave of the hand. "I can take care of myself."

"Mh…"

"I can do it in my spare time if you want! I have some vacation racked up."

He studied her keenly, eyes sparkling with mirth. "Tell you what. You make sure you win this thing. Cause as far as I can tell, no winner of the show has been snatched, right?"

"Is that why you're so worried?" She laughed. "You think I'll allow one of those musclebound idiots to seduce me? Fat chance!"

"It's not you I'm worried about, sweetheart," said Dan, real concern lacing his voice.

She gaped at her editor, aghast. "You think… Chase will fall for some painted bimbo?"

"He's a man, Odelia," her editor declared solemnly, "and men are weak."

"Not Chase. Uh-uh. Plus, we're getting married in September."

"Exactly. A man who's about to be tied down for life is like a cat on a hot tin roof. He's liable to make some very strange moves."

She shook her head. "Nope. No way. Chase would never cheat on me."

"If you say so."

"I *am* saying so! Chase doesn't even *look* at other women. He's absolutely faithful, and I have complete faith in him."

Dan spread his arms. "Looks like you've got all your bases covered."

"You mean… it's a go?"

He smiled. "It's a go." But then he raised his finger, like a schoolteacher about to dispense some nuggets of wisdom. "Just promise me you won't put yourself in danger, and the moment you see anyone act suspicious, tell Kimmy, so she can send in the cavalry."

"Well, let's hope the cavalry, in the form of Chase, won't be too busy with his harem of seductresses to come running when the call goes out," said Odelia with a grin.

Dan nodded seriously. "Let's hope so."

"I was kidding!"

"I was not," said Dan. "For a couple that's about to tie the knot, the last thing I would advise is to participate in a show like Passion Island."

"Don't worry, Dan," said Odelia as she got up. "Both Chase and I are professionals. This is just a job for us, not an opportunity to go wild."

But as she left the office, she had the impression Dan still wasn't fully on board with the scheme. And she had to admit that his attitude had sown the first seeds of doubt in her mind. Maybe Dan was right. Subjecting Chase to six seasoned seductresses—some of the most beautiful women on the planet—eager to do anything and everything in their power to lure him into their beds, maybe wasn't the best idea for a man about to say 'I do.'

But then she shrugged off Dan's misgivings. The man was old and cynical. That's what you got from being a newspaperman for forty years. You got jaded.

Chase would be fine, and so would she, and she'd get one hell of a story out of the whole thing. Even if Kimmy was wrong, and no foul play was involved, she'd still get the inside scoop on one of the most popular reality shows in recent times.

Three weeks in a tropical paradise, all expenses paid. Yippie!

9

*A*s is our custom, we dropped by the office to regale Odelia with the latest tidbits of news from the streets of Hampton Cove. It wasn't all that earth-shattering, but still. Buster, the hairdresser's Main Coon, told us that Gwayn Partington, the plumber, was having an affair with the electrician's wife, and that Mayor Butterwick had decided to adopt a new hairstyle. Over at the police precinct we'd witnessed firsthand how Uncle Alec had been looking up websites on hair transplants and had taken receipt of a box of Slimmo, the patented method of losing up to thirty pounds in a single week. And at the doctor's office Tex's replacement Denby Jennsen was still as popular as ever, his waiting room filled with half of Hampton Cove's female population. Jennsen is a very handsome man, it must be said, and could probably snag a major part in any medical TV show.

Denby's Anatomy, in other words, was very much in demand.

So all in all not much news, and certainly nothing worth

printing, unless Odelia decided to turn the budding romance between her uncle and Charlene Butterwick into newspaper fodder, turning them into a local celebrity couple. Somehow I didn't think the affair between the town's mayor and chief of police would capture the hearts and minds to the same extent as some Hollywood heartthrob's latest conquest, though.

"Great news, you guys," said Odelia the moment we walked into her office.

"We have some great news, too," said Dooley. "Uncle Alec is getting new hair and a new waistline."

This stymied Odelia somewhat. "What?" she asked, taken aback a little.

I explained to her about Slimmo and the hair transplant site and Odelia tsk-tsked mildly. "You shouldn't spy on my uncle or my uncle's girlfriend, you guys."

And here I thought she wanted us to spy on everyone. "Also, Charlene asked Fido to give her Jennifer Aniston's hair," said Dooley, not discouraged by Odelia's admonition.

Odelia frowned as she processed this. "Mh. So Charlene got Jennifer Aniston's haircut and my uncle is surfing hair transplant websites and taking dodgy diet pills. I have a feeling their romance is seriously hotting up."

"He was also surfing some other site," said Dooley. He crinkled his brow as he tried to recall. "They sell little blue pills that help men with their election. Do you think Uncle Alec is going to enter the election, Odelia?"

Odelia blushed a little, and appeared flustered by this information. I would have corrected Dooley, but somehow I had a feeling this would lead me into hot water, so I didn't.

Odelia cleared her throat. "In other news," she said, "I think you'll be happy to know that Dan has given me the green light."

Dooley appeared puzzled. "Why would Dan give you a green light?"

"I mean, he gave me the go-ahead."

"Go ahead where?"

"Thailand! And you guys are coming with!"

I don't think I've ever seen a cat turn white around the nostrils. For one thing it's very hard to notice, what with all the hair, but I had the distinct impression Dooley went as white as a sheet. "But I don't want to go!" he cried, once he'd recovered from the shock.

"What?" said Odelia, taken aback by his vehemence.

"They eat cats in Thailand, Odelia," he lamented, "and I don't want to be eaten!"

She laughed—actually had the gall to laugh at our predicament! I'd always thought Odelia was a compassionate person, always looking out for our well-being. But now, certain death staring us in the face, she was practically rolling on the floor laughing!

"People don't eat cats in Thailand, Dooley," she said once she'd recovered from her laughing fit. "That's China you're thinking about."

"No, I'm not thinking about China," said Dooley. "I'm thinking about Thailand and the fact that I don't want to be roasted over a slow fire like a chicken."

"Rotisserie cat," I said in a low voice, and shivered from stem to stern. "Brrr."

"Look, you guys, no one is going to roast you over a fire, slow or otherwise. I'm sure the Thai simply love cats—they revere them. So you'll be perfectly safe. And I'll be there with you the whole time, so nothing can happen. In fact, since I'm one of the candidates, I'm pretty sure I'll be treated like royalty over there. And that means so will you."

"Royalty?" asked Dooley, still suspicious. "Are you sure?"

"Of course I'm sure! Passion Island is the network's

biggest moneymaker, so they're going to make sure we're pampered to within an inch of our lives. And you know what that means. The best hotel, the best food, the best accommodations. In fact it wouldn't surprise me if you two didn't get your own personal assistant to cater to your every need."

I perked up at this, and so did Dooley. A personal assistant catering to our every need was just the kind of thing I'd always dreamed of. Odelia may be the best human a cat could find, but she's also a very busy human, always running off to cover some story or try and solve some mystery, rarely taking the time to pamper us twenty-four seven.

"When are we leaving?" asked Dooley, having come around to the idea of going to Thailand in record time.

"I'll have to confirm with Kimmy, but I think we're expected to travel in a couple of days. They'd selected another couple, but they've had to drop out, on account of the fact that the woman turned out to be pregnant."

"They don't like pregnant women on the show?" I asked.

"No, that's where they draw the line. They don't mind breaking up couples, but not couples that are married, or pregnant. They're not that cruel. So Kimmy managed to slot us in, since they needed a new couple last minute." She grabbed her phone. "I have to tell Chase. He needs to talk to my uncle about taking a leave of absence."

"What about Harriet and Brutus?" I asked.

"What about them?" said Odelia distractedly as she typed a message on her phone, fingers darting across the screen with a dexterity that was close to the speed of light.

"Are they also going to Thailand?"

"Nope. When I told Kimmy I wanted to bring my pets she wasn't keen. She only relented when I made it clear I wasn't going without you, but she drew the line at two. If I took Harriet and Brutus I'd look more like a crazy cat lady and less like a candidate for Passion Island. Gran will take care of Harriet and Brutus while we're away."

I shared a look of concern with Dooley. Somehow I had the feeling this wouldn't go down well with Harriet. Not well at all.

"**W**hat do you mean I can't go?" Gran cried. She stood, hands on hips, looking the picture of distress and disappointment.

"I'm sorry, Gran, but it's a miracle Kimmy managed to get me and Chase on the show. There's no way she could extend the courtesy to other members of my family."

"What other members? I'm your sidekick. I'm the Dr. Watson to your Sherlock Holmes, the Hastings to your Poirot, the Jake to your Fatman—not that you're fat."

"It's just another investigation, Gran," said Odelia. "You'd be bored to tears."

"Bored to tears on Passion Island? Are you nuts? It's the adventure of a lifetime, the thing I've been dreaming of!"

They were in Odelia's living room, Jeopardy playing in the background, and an aproned Chase preparing dinner in the kitchen—spaghetti bolognese, his specialty.

"You're not going to leave your poor old granny at home, are you?" asked Gran, lip quivering and voice breaking. "All alone in this big old house with no one to take care of me?"

"Harriet and Brutus will be here," Odelia pointed out. "And I've asked Uncle Alec to drop by every day."

"It's not the same and you know it," said Gran, sinking down onto the couch. "Besides, Alec is so busy wining and dining Charlene these days he'll forget about his poor old mother the moment you take off for the airport." Next to Gran on the couch, two more disappointed members of Odelia's family sat. Reading left to right, they were Harriet and Brutus. Though Brutus didn't look half as disappointed as Harriet. In fact Odelia had the impression Brutus didn't mind one bit. Harriet, though, looked crestfallen.

"I love that show, Odelia," said the Persian. "In fact it's the one show that could really benefit from my presence."

Harriet had told Odelia all about her idea to launch a second Passion Island show, this time focusing on cats. Odelia didn't see how that was even remotely possible, but it just goes to show that Harriet loved Passion Island with a passion bordering on obsession. It pained Odelia to have to leave them behind, but there was simply no way she could talk Kimmy into providing accommodation for two more of her cats.

"I'm sorry," she said. "But it's only for a short time. We'll be back before you know it."

"Why don't you take me and leave Max?" Harriet suggested now. "I mean, I'm just as much of a sleuth as he is, and he doesn't even like Passion Island. I do. I know everything there is to know about that show."

"Don't waste your breath, honey," said Gran as she morosely stared at Alex Trebek. "Can't you see her mind is made up? My favorite granddaughter has decided to stab her nearest and dearest in the back, all for the chance of becoming a star."

"Gran, it's not like that," said Odelia.

"Oh, no?" The old lady pointed a bony finger in her

granddaughter's direction. "The moment you're selected for Passion Island you cruelly ditch your sickly old grandmother and your two favorite cats. You know what I call that? Diva behavior. You're not the same person you once were, Odelia. Success has gone to your head. It's made you hard. In fact, you know what?" She got up very swiftly for a sickly old lady, and made for the sliding glass door. "I don't think I want to see you for a while. I'm going back to my own home. Alone. Without anyone to love me or care for me." And with a stifled sob, she slowly closed the door, stared at Odelia for a few moments, then slumped her shoulders and slouched off.

"Maybe we can find a way to bring her along?" Odelia suggested now, her heart breaking at the sight of her gran.

"Don't fall for it," said Chase. "She's just putting on an act."

"You think so?"

"Sure." Chase smiled and pressed a kiss to her temple. "I haven't known your gran as long as you have, obviously, but even I can tell when she's faking it."

"Still…"

"She's better off here. If what Kimmy suspects is true, the set of Passion Island is the last place she should be. That place is dangerous."

Odelia nodded and put placemats on the table.

"Besides, I'll bet she'll be back here in five minutes."

"She will?"

"Sure. The woman loves my spaghetti."

❧

That night, Odelia talked to her parents on Skype. She was happy to see how well they looked.

"Thailand?" asked her dad. "Are you sure, honey? I've

44

heard terrible stories about those reality shows. And participants disappearing? That doesn't sound like the thing you should get involved in."

"Kimmy doesn't have anywhere else to turn, Dad," she said. "And I'm sure the set will be a safe place. The participants only disappeared once the show was already taped."

"I love Passion Island," said her mother, not surprisingly. "In fact I've asked your grandmother to record the reruns. I hope she hasn't forgotten."

"Oh, I doubt it," said Dad. "Not now that her granddaughter will be one of the participants." He smiled broadly. In spite of his qualms, he was clearly proud of his daughter. "And you're telling me Chase will also be there?"

"Yeah, we're going as a couple."

"And the idea is…"

"Oh, Tex," said Mom, giving her husband a light slap on the shoulder. "I've told you a million times how it works. Four couples go to Thailand, then are separated. The men on one island and the women on another. Six seducers then try to seduce the women, and six seductresses try to seduce the men. The couple that manages to stay together, wins."

"But why?" asked Tex. "What's the point?"

"It's a reality show!" said Odelia laughingly. "Does there really have to be a point?"

Dad was shaking his head. "So six men are going to try and seduce you?"

"Yeah, and six of the most gorgeous women are going to try and seduce Chase." As she spoke the words, Dan's reservations echoed in her ears. She decided to ignore them.

"I don't know, honey. Still sounds like a bad idea if you ask me," said Dad.

"What sounds like a bad idea, Dad?" asked Chase, pulling up a chair.

Dad winced. Lately Chase had started calling him 'Dad' and for some reason it grated on the good doctor. "So, um, how is Denby doing?" he asked, abruptly changing the topic.

"Oh, he's fine," said Odelia. "I dropped by this afternoon and he said he's never been busier. He didn't know Hampton Cove had so many sick people."

"Sick women, you mean," said Chase. "Since he took over for Dad the number of women has multiplied, and I don't think it's because they've all suddenly developed some life-threatening disease, either." He laughed. "He's one handsome devil, that Denby, Dad. Aren't you worried he'll take over your office and settle down permanently?"

"Denby would never do that," said Dad stoically. "So, Chase, how do you feel about this whole Passion Island gag?"

Chase suddenly turned serious. Odelia had often noticed that her fiancé had two faces: his regular, laidback demeanor, and his cop face, which he pulled when he talked shop. As if some inner switch was flipped and his well-honed police instincts took over. "I think the whole thing stinks," he said now. "Five women disappearing and the producers don't even want to investigate? Something is pretty rotten, Dad."

"Please," said Dad, in a slightly strangled voice. "Just... call me Tex?"

"But why, Dad? We're family now."

"Just... humor me, will you?"

Chase shrugged, but Odelia could tell he wasn't happy about it. "Sure... Tex."

Abruptly the tall cop got up and stalked off.

"Where did he go?" asked Dad, surprised.

"Where do you think? You just told him not to call you dad," said Odelia.

"How could you, Tex?" said Mom. "Chase loves you and you had to go and break his heart."

"I didn't break his heart! I just don't like it when people call me dad that aren't my flesh and blood."

"Tex!"

"What?!"

"Yeah, Dad, that wasn't very nice of you," said Odelia.

"It sounds weird!"

"Well, get used to it, cause Chase is going to be in our lives a lot from now on," said Mom.

"Oh, all right. He can call me dad. Happy now?"

"Don't say it if you don't mean it, Tex," said Mom.

"I mean it! I do!"

"Then you better tell Chase. And apologize."

"Chase!" Odelia called out. "Dad wants to tell you something!"

Chase came ambling up, hands stuffed into his pockets, his face a thundercloud. "What?" he asked sullenly as he reluctantly sat down again, then studied his fingernails.

"Chase, son," said Dad, "I'm sorry about before. I want you to call me dad from now on."

"I thought you wanted me to call you Tex?" Chase grumbled.

"Well, I'd love it if you called me dad," said Dad. "Absolutely love it." He winced a little, then said, "I was worried you wouldn't want to. And I didn't want you to feel obligated."

Chase's face lit up. "I don't mind. In fact I love it. Dad."

Dad grimaced, then managed an ingratiating smile. "That's the spirit. Son."

"We're one big happy family," said Mom. "And that's just the way we like it."

"One big happy family but I'm not included," Gran muttered as she walked by on her way to the stairs.

"Ma!" mom yelled, but Gran ignored her. "What did she say just now?"

"Oh, she's mad because she doesn't get to go to Thailand," Odelia explained.

"She'll get over it," Mom said. "Now there's one thing I want to tell Chase before we sign off. Whatever happens in Thailand—"

"Stays in Thailand," Dad said with a grin, earning himself another slap from Mom.

"Whatever happens, Chase, remember one thing."

Odelia smiled as she fully expected her mother to tell Chase that his future wife loved him, and that no seductresses could ever come between him and true love.

Instead, Mom said: "There are infrared cameras in the bedrooms capturing your every move. In fact they've got cameras hooked up all over the island."

"Oh-kay," said Chase, a little startled.

"Mom!" said Odelia. "Chase doesn't need to know about the cameras because there's not going to be anything worth filming. Isn't that right, Chase? Honey?"

"No, of course, of course," said Chase, a little too quickly, Odelia felt.

Dad suddenly leaned closer to the screen. "I also got something to tell you, son." The upper half of his face now filled the screen. "If you cheat on my daughter you never get to call me dad ever again, is that understood?"

"I understand, sir," said Chase soberly.

"I mean it, son. If you ever so much as lay a hand on one of those sedu—"

But the connection cut out before he could finish his sentence. Possibly because Mom and Dad had bad Wi-Fi in the hotel in Rome where they were currently holed up, or— more likely, Odelia felt—because Mom had ended the conversation, not wanting Dad to start threatening Chase with grievous bodily harm.

And not for the first time since she'd accepted the assignment, a tiny sliver of doubt entered Odelia's mind. And when she opened the email Kimmy had sent, containing pictures of all six seductresses, those doubts only multiplied.

These women were every man's wet dream.

She just hoped they weren't Chase's.

*C*ats don't fly. That's always been my contention and I stick to it. We're not built for being hurled through infinite space in a narrow metal tube. Still, if we're compelled to fly, on account of the fact that our human doesn't take no for an answer, best to do it in style.

And it has to be said: Sunshine Pictures had spared no expense to transport its contestants from one part of the world to the other. On the flight over, Dooley and I even had our own cubicle where we were being pampered to our hearts' content.

"Air travel is starting to grow on me, Max," said Dooley once we were well underway. We'd just tucked into our bowls of gourmet lasagna—Garfield-approved, no doubt—and a very nice young lady had fluffed up our cushions to perfection, and as we gazed out at the deck of clouds below, the plane's powerful engines taking us ever closer to the land of the Thai, I endorsed my friend's view wholeheartedly.

"It doesn't really feel as if we're hundreds of feet in the air," I said.

"And those clouds look like soft pillows," he said, a little lazily. "So if we fall from the sky, we'll probably land very softly."

"We won't even feel a thing."

"Just a very smooth sensation of landing on top a giant ball of cotton."

Suddenly, the intercom crackled to life and the captain's voice croaked, "Be advised that we're approaching some minor turbulence. Please fasten your seatbelts."

And even before the words were out of the man's mouth, suddenly the plane dropped from the sky and my stomach collided with my teeth.

"Max!" Dooley cried. "We're going to dieeeeeeeeee!"

I would have dissuaded him from this bleak view hadn't I taken the same view myself. "This is the end!" I cried, as my friend clasped his paws around my, admittedly, pudgy midsection.

"Max, you're my best friend and I love you so much!" Dooley tooted in my ear.

"Likewise, Dooley. I love you, buddy!"

The plane suddenly lurched, and both Dooley and I were swept up into the air and almost hit the ceiling, before returning with a plop to our cushioned seats. Meanwhile, we both yelled our little heads off.

"I once ate a piece of kibble that belonged to you, Max!" Dooley said, having entered the confession stage of this impending-doom scenario.

"I forgive you!" I returned.

"And I once peed in Brutus's water bowl after he said some nasty things about you!"

"Oh, Dooley!"

"He told me later his water tasted funny and thought it was ozone."

I laughed, and so did Dooley. And then, as unexpectedly as it had started, the plane steadied, and the captain announced that the 'mild' turbulence was a thing of the past.

"Um, Dooley?" I said after a moment's pause.

"Yes, Max?"

"You can let go of me now."

"Oh, all right."

Odelia popped her head into our little cubicle. "Are you guys all right?"

"I thought we were going to die," Dooley confessed.

"Me, too," I said.

She smiled. "You didn't die, and you're not going to. Now try to get some rest. It's still a couple of hours before we land."

She withdrew, leaving us to ruminate on our most recent brush with death.

"Max?"

"Mh?"

"I don't think I like airplanes all that much after all."

"Me, neither."

I must have fallen asleep then, for when I woke up the plane was already landing. We'd arrived in Thailand, and our new adventure had begun.

The moment we were off the plane, a fancy black car took us to our hotel, where Odelia proceeded to introduce us to our room. The next day we were traveling to the island that would be our home for the next couple of weeks. But for now we were in five-star lodgings in the heart of Bangkok, which is Thailand's capital, and probably its most famous city.

As I gazed out of the hotel room window, I saw a hubbub of life outside. Little cars called rickshaws or Tuk-tuks criss-crossed the streets, and it appeared as if there were people and cars and buses everywhere.

"This looks a lot busier than Hampton Cove," Dooley remarked.

"Yes, it certainly does," I agreed.

I also saw plenty of dogs that didn't seem to belong to anyone, and wondered briefly if the rumors about the Thai eating cats and dogs weren't true, after all. At least they couldn't eat us, ensconced as we were in our fancy hotel room.

"Let's go out," Odelia announced.

"Are you sure? I'm pretty bushed," Chase replied, indicating her words hadn't been meant for Dooley and myself.

"Yeah, I've never been to Bangkok before. We should take this opportunity to see something of the city."

"As you wish," said Chase with a smile.

Odelia crouched down next to us. "Will you guys be all right in here?"

"Oh, sure," I said, and stifled a yawn. In spite of the fact that I'd slept on the plane, I was ready for another nap. "You and Chase have a good time," I said encouragingly. "Dooley and I will nap until you get back."

She petted my head and then they were off, leaving us in the relative silence of our room on the fourth floor of the hotel.

And it has to be said, I slept like a log, and didn't even notice when Odelia and Chase returned.

"It's jet lag," Dooley knew when we both woke up in the middle of the night. "I saw it on the Discovery Channel. Your body travels through several time zones and it takes a while to catch up."

We were both curled up on the foot of the bed, and as I listened to the combined snores of Odelia and Chase, it felt just like home.

I woke up again from the sound of footfalls on the carpet and opened my eyes to see what was going on.

In the darkness of the room, I suddenly saw that a man was standing there. He was at the foot of the bed, holding up a phone and it looked as if he was filming us.

I gulped a little, and poked Odelia's foot. She stirred, and I whispered, "There's someone standing there filming us!"

"Yes, Mom," she murmured. "I promise I'll be a good girl."

"Chase, wake up!" I said, giving the cop's foot a prod.

"The name is Bond. Chase Bond," Chase mumbled.

"There's an intruder!" I loud-whispered, to no avail.

The intruder must have gotten hip to the fact that a cat was following his every move, and what sounded to Odelia's ears as actual words forming coherent sentences must have sounded to him like plaintive mewling.

So even before I managed to rouse my human from sleep, the man lowered his phone and tip-toed away again.

I hopped down from the bed, eager to go in pursuit and find out what was going on, but as I reached the door, he closed it, and that put a stop to my attempts to play detective.

Before he shut the door, though, I caught a glimpse of his face. A scar sliced his left eyebrow, giving him a very sinister aspect indeed.

As I returned to the bed, this time eager to alert my human of the dastardly deeds in progress, she opened her eyes and, after I'd told her my tale, smiled and said, "Go back to sleep, Max. You're just having a nightmare, that's all."

"But he was right here!" I cried.

"That's great," she mumbled, and tumbled into a deep sleep, setting an example for me to follow.

Unfortunately I wasn't convinced it had been a nightmare. In fact I was pretty sure it had been a real person. But I was so tired that soon sleep came, regardless of my vigilance, and when Scarface returned, it was in my dreams, just as Odelia had said. Only in my dream he wasn't holding up a smartphone but a dead cat. And as he opened his mouth, showcasing two neat rows of razor-sharp teeth, he growled, "I could eat a horse!" But instead of a horse, he ate the cat instead!

I returned to wakefulness with a yelp, only to be greeted by the sight of Chase prancing around the room in his boxers and announcing, "I could eat a horse!" to anyone who would listen.

"What's wrong, Max?" asked Dooley. "You look like you've seen a ghost."

After I'd told him my tale of woe and sorrow—or rather our nocturnal visitor—he stared at me, wide-eyed and fearful.

"A catnapper!" he cried. "He was here to catnap and eat us, Max!"

"I'm pretty sure he didn't have any intention of eating us," I assured my friend.

"But then what was he doing here?"

"I have no idea." I glanced at my human, who was sitting up and yawning, looking pretty bedraggled. Even under normal circumstances Odelia isn't a morning person, but now she looked as if she'd gone through several spin cycles in a washing machine. So I decided to wait to tell her what had happened until she'd had her breakfast.

Still, it was a portentous way to start our trip. Nocturnal visitors filming us while we were sleeping? Not good!

*B*reakfast was also an opportunity to meet some of the members of the production team. Kimmy was there, of course, but also her boss, Clint Bunda, a barrel-chested man with a head shaped like a bullet and gleaming like one, too. Either he'd had a close shave, or he was naturally hairless. Odelia was greeted with a cordial handshake, and so was Chase.

"I'm so glad Kimmy found you," said Clint as he put his feet under the table. "I don't know what I would have done without you. The couple who were supposed to come turned out to be married *and* pregnant! Which of course is strictly against the rules."

"Well, we're neither married nor pregnant," said Chase, earning himself a laugh from the producer.

"Have the other couples arrived already?" asked Odelia.

"Yeah, I think they'll be here soon," he said, twisting his head to scan the dining room. "That couple over there is part of the lineup," he said as he gestured to a young couple seated at one of the tables.

"They're very young," said Odelia.

"Yeah, most participants are," said Clint. "Not everyone wants to jeopardize their relationship this way. The younger the more adventurous, and also the less invested in their relationship, of course. How long have you guys been together?"

"Three years," said Odelia.

"Long time," said the producer, nodding as he sedulously buttered his bagel. "And still willing to risk it all, huh?"

"Yeah, we're planning to get married soon," Chase explained, repeating the story they'd rehearsed. "And we figured the prize money would come in handy."

Clint chuckled. "Getting married can cost an arm and a leg. I would know. My daughter got married last year, and it pretty much ruined me. I told her if she ever gets divorced, she's going to pay me back—with interest!"

"Ha ha," said Chase obligingly.

"Ha ha," said Odelia pleasantly.

The only one who wasn't laughing was Kimmy. She probably was used to her boss's peculiar sense of humor.

The dining room was filling up quickly, and Odelia eyed the breakfast buffet eagerly.

"Don't worry," said Kimmy, leaning in as she caught Odelia's look. "There's plenty."

She laughed. "How did you know what I was thinking?"

"Because I thought the same thing when I first came out here. This hotel is one of the best in the city."

"We went out last night and I have to say the nightlife is impressive," she said.

"I know. Did you go to Khao San Road?"

"We did! I don't think I've ever seen so many people having such a good time."

She and Chase had both been pretty tired, but had still walked around for an hour or so before returning to their hotel. The flashy lights, music and people everywhere had been intoxicating, and it was obvious Bangkok was a city that never slept—unlike them.

"The weirdest thing happened last night," said Odelia the moment Clint had gotten up to chat with the other couple. "I woke up in the middle of the night and I could have sworn there was someone in the room with us, filming us with his smartphone. When I called out, he quickly disappeared."

Kimmy frowned thoughtfully. "Are you sure?"

"Pretty sure." She wasn't, of course, still convinced it had simply been Max having a nightmare. When he'd repeated his story that morning, and added he'd had a real nightmare later on, this time featuring a cat-eating villainous figure, she'd been even more inclined to favor the nightmare story. Then again, Max was no fool. If he said he'd seen someone, it was better to check.

"Do you think there's a way to see who it was?" she asked. "Security cameras in the corridor, maybe, or even the room?"

"I'll ask hotel security," said Kimmy, nodding. "I don't think there's cameras in the rooms, for reasons of privacy, but the hallways and corridors are probably watched."

She got up, and so did Odelia. She'd been eyeing those little muffins and other pastries for a long time, and finally couldn't resist the urge. And as she walked over, a young couple entered the dining room and glanced around. He was sporting an intricately cut hairstyle, with what looked like a name razored on the side of his head. It spelled 'Hot Dude.' He also was wearing shades and a tank top that showcased his chiseled physique. She was blond, extremely tan, and had a nose ring. In her daisy dukes and crop top she looked like the perfect candidate for Passion Island.

Odelia smiled in their direction, and opened her mouth to introduce herself, when they both pointedly ignored her and walked the other way.

Odelia retracted her proffered hand and shrugged. She

wasn't here to make friends, but it would have been nice to find some, considering she and Chase were going to be separated soon, and not even allowed a cell phone.

As she piled her plate with those tiny pastries, the female half of the couple Clint had pointed out to them followed her example.

"Are you also here for Passion Island?" asked the woman, sounding nervous.

She was a brunette, with her hair in a ponytail, and looked pretty but a little plain, at least in comparison to the other couple.

"Yes, I am," said Odelia.

"Oh, great," said the woman, and held out her hand. "I'm Tina, and that guy over there eating his body weight in sausages is Nick."

Odelia," said Odelia, and gestured to her table. "And that's Chase."

"He looks fit," said Tina, and immediately looked mortified. "Oh, heck, I said that out loud, didn't I? I mean, he looks nice."

"And fit," said Odelia with a smile. "He's not a seducer, though, so you won't be seeing him, I'm afraid."

"Oh, no, I didn't mean it like that!" said the woman, her cheeks coloring. "I'm sorry. I don't know why I said that. I guess I'm not used to this kind of thing. Seducers and seductresses and all of that stuff. This wasn't my idea, you know. It was all Nick. He pretty much had to drag me here kicking and screaming," She rolled her eyes. "Men."

"So why did you agree?"

"Well, Nick said this would be the ultimate relationship test for us. We're getting married in the fall, see." She showed a neat little engagement ring, proudly holding it out for Odelia's inspection. "And Nick thought it would be a good idea to make sure there were no doubts. I'm a pretty jealous kind of gal, and I've been giving Nick hell, I'm afraid. He's got a pretty extensive circle of friends, a lot of them women. And so I get insecure. And he just figured we'd settle this once and for all, and he'd prove to me that he loves me and he's not going to cheat on me. And 50.000 prize money sounds pretty sweet."

"Yeah, that's the main reason we're doing this," Odelia confided, reiterating her rehearsed storyline. "We're getting married in September, and that money would be a nice down payment for a house."

"Oh, you lucky girl!" Tina cried, then held her hand to her mouth again. "I keep blurting out the most inappropriate things, don't I?"

"It's all right," said Odelia, laughing.

They both watched as Nick was approached by the female half of the other couple, and immediately his face lit up and he started making animated conversation.

Next to Odelia, Tina sighed. "See what I mean? He can't see a woman or he has to chat her up."

Odelia nodded, and felt for Tina. She had the impression she wouldn't go home with the big prize. But instead, she said, "I'm sure he's just being friendly."

But from the way Nick's eyes kept dropping down the woman's crop top and checking out her enhanced chest, friendly probably wasn't the right word.

13

*O*delia had arranged for Dooley and me to be treated to a breakfast as hearty as the one she and Chase were getting. Which meant... room service! Now if there's one thing I love about traveling it's this very concept of room service. Of course you could say that us cats enjoy room service all of our lives, but the service at a hotel is still a little different from the one at home. I don't know if it's the food, or being far from home, but overall it's a pleasant experience. Especially if the room service person is as friendly as the one who'd delivered our breakfast—a sweet lady with extremely kind demeanor.

So we thanked our benefactor, even though she probably couldn't understand a meow we said, and dug into our juicy fillets and sauce-covered nuggets with relish.

And it was as we devoured the treats that the door opened again and a man strode in.

"More room service!" Dooley cried happily. "Oh, Max, my bones are going to become as big as yours if this keeps up!"

I gave him a look of extreme censure, which went straight over his head, as he was too busy eagerly anticipating this new person's gifts, and so I turned my attention in the same direction.

And got the shock of a lifetime.

The man who'd just entered... was the same man from last night.

"It's the guy!" I cried.

"I know!" said Dooley. "I hope he's brought pâté. I love pâté."

"No, I mean it's the same guy from last night. The intruder!"

Dooley's jaw dropped. "What does he want!" he cried.

It soon became clear what the man wanted: to snoop.

He went straight for Odelia's laptop, which she'd left on the table, and opened it. His hands were gloved, and his fingers were soon deftly probing the keyboard. Judging from the look of frustration on his face, though, Odelia's password gave him pause.

So instead, he started searching around, until he found her iPad.

"We have to do something," I said. "He's going to steal Odelia's tablet!"

"But what can we do!" said Dooley. "He's a lot bigger and a lot stronger than us!"

"He doesn't know we're here," I said. "Maybe we can scare him away."

Dooley blinked. It was obvious he wasn't fully on board with my plan. Heck, I wasn't fully on board with my plan, and it was my own plan! This man had featured in my nightmare, stringing up a cat and threatening to eat it, so I wasn't exactly eager to make his acquaintance. But we couldn't stand idly by and watch him burgle the room, either.

So with a loud meow, I burst onto the scene.

The man looked up, startled at the sight and sound of

yours truly. What he didn't do, though, even though I'd hoped he would, was turn tail and run to the nearest exit.

Instead, he growled, "Get lost, you filthy animal."

Now if there's one thing I don't like it's to be called a filthy animal. Like most cats I take pride in my sense of personal hygiene. I primp, I prink, and sometimes I even preen.

"I'm not a filthy animal," I told the man. "You're the filthy animal. Coming in here and stealing Odelia's tablet."

But he wasn't to be deterred. I guess that's where dogs have it easier. If they're big enough, and loud enough, they can scare any burglarious individual away simply by stepping onto the scene. Whereas cats have that cuddly, endearing image going for them. Not exactly the way to go when faced with an element of the criminal classes.

It was at this moment that Dooley finally overcame his natural tendency towards timidity, and leaped onto the scene with a loud hiss, his tail distended and his back arched.

"Yikes!" the intruder yelped at the sight of my friend. But instead of beating a retreat, as any sane man would have done, he still found the time to check Odelia's tablet.

"It's not working, Max," said Dooley. "He doesn't seem to be impressed."

"I think we have to attack, Dooley," I said.

"Attack?"

"Yeah, claws out and attack!" I instructed, leading by example.

I don't know if you've ever been attacked by a cat? I can assure you it's not a pleasant experience. We may be cuddly and cute, renowned for our lovable persona and sweet-natured companionship, but when the gloves are off, we can do some real damage.

It's all in the claws, you see. They're pretty sharp, and

when applied with precision and intent, can dig deep in places you wouldn't expect.

Like someone's thigh.

So as Dooley attacked the man's right thigh, and I dug my claws into the left, the man screamed both in surprise and agony, as he desperately tried to dislodge us from his person.

I wasn't to be deterred, though, and neither was Dooley. My friend may be the sweetest cat on the planet, but once he's going well, it's hard to make him stop.

And it was as I clawed my way up from the man's thigh to his nether regions, pretty much treating the intruder like I would a tree or scratching post, that he threw in the towel, and with a blood-curdling scream—his blood, not mine—made for the door, hindered somewhat by two cats dangling from the lower strata of his corpus.

As he reached the door, he made a swiping motion with his hands, and sent both myself and Dooley flying, but not before a ripping sound indicated we'd done our bit, turning his nice jeans into mere strips of torn fabric flapping around the man's legs.

As is our wont, we landed on our feet, and watched with a measure of satisfaction as the man slammed the door, after hurling a certain measure of abuse in our direction.

Sticks and stones, though, right? And at least we'd achieved our objective: Odelia's personal possessions had been safeguarded, and Scarface had been outfitted with a few more scars for his collection.

"My heart," said Dooley, panting as loudly as I did. "It's beating so fast, Max!"

"Yeah, that's normal," I said. My heart was practically hammering through my chest, too. "It's the adrenaline," I told Dooley.

"It tastes funny," said Dooley now, as he licked his claw.

"That's blood," I said.

Dooley gulped a little. "Blood!"

But before we could thresh the matter out more thoroughly, the room door opened again, and this time Odelia and Chase walked in. And as we regaled them with the story of our recent heroics, Odelia didn't look happy. Not happy at all. Nor could I blame her. If strange men with scarred faces enter your room not once but twice in a short space of time, it's enough to give you pause.

Of course, we were in a strange town in a strange country. It was entirely possible that breaking into rooms to go through people's personal possessions and taking pictures while they're sleeping is some sort of local custom. All part of the Bangkok experience.

Though somehow, judging from Odelia's reaction, and Chase's, I didn't think so.

14

*O*delia and Chase didn't have time to investigate the break-in properly, as at eleven on the dot they were expected downstairs in the lobby. Surrounded by cameras, the four couples were expected to enact the second scene of the sixth season of Passion Island: the teary goodbye.

The first scene had been the interview Kimmy had set up, which had taken place in their hotel room. They'd talked a little about themselves, their history as a couple, and what they expected from their participation in the show.

Max and Dooley had both been relegated to their respective cages, something which they absolutely abhorred but which was necessary for the trip to the island, and as Odelia and Chase hammed it up for the cameras, Odelia even managing to squeeze a couple of tears from her eyes like a seasoned actress, she had the impression that the other couples didn't even have to fake it. Tina and Nick were bawling like babies, and even the tough-looking blonde was crying her eyes out, even if her other half wasn't. The fourth couple, whom she only saw now for the first time, was a plain-looking pair. The girl, named Joanna, was a freckle-faced pretty redhead, and her boyfriend was a chubby-looking young man who could have been a sales manager in an insurance company.

She understood now what Kimmy had told her about the selection process Clint employed: they tried to get people whom the public could identify with. So when they failed to stay together, the viewers at home would be as thrown as the cheated partner.

Chase held her close, and whispered, "Talk to you soon, babe... on our secret phone."

She smiled. Kimmy had promised to sneak them a phone, so they could stay in touch. All they needed to do was make sure Clint didn't catch them.

"I feel like a spy going on a secret mission," she said.

"It'll be fine," said Chase. "Though I'm still not entirely sure this is such a good idea."

"Why?"

"You're the one running the risk. It's not the men they target but the women."

He was right, of course. That and Scarface lurking around their hotel room was enough to give Odelia the heebie-jeebies.

Kimmy had talked to security, but unfortunately the cameras in that section of the hotel had suffered an electrical failure. Coincidence? Somehow she didn't think so.

"If anything happens, you can always swim to the rescue," she quipped.

Chase grinned. "Just say the word, babe, and I'm on my way."

The two islands—Koh Samui for the women and Koh Phangan for the men—were separated by a nineteen-mile strip of sea that could be crossed by ferry in half an hour. Swimming, unfortunately, wasn't recommended, both for the distance—about the same distance as the English Channel between Calais and Dover—and the many sharks infesting the Gulf of Thailand, where both islands were located.

"I'll find a boat," Chase assured her when she reminded him of this fact. "And there's always Kimmy. She'll keep an eye on you, too."

Kimmy was their ally in this, their most peculiar adventure yet, or at least the most exotic.

"Time to go!" Clint called out, checking his watch.

"Stay safe, babe," said Chase as he planted a kiss on her lips.

"You, too, and don't let the seductresses bite," she added for good measure.

He grinned. "Don't worry. *I only have eyes for you...*" he sang, out of tune as usual. It still managed to put a smile on her face, and then the men were led out by one of Clint's people, and the women by Kimmy, the men filing into a black van and the women into a white one, and then they were off...

"How come we're coming with you?" asked Dooley from his cage, sat at her feet. "I mean, Max and I are both males, so shouldn't we be going to the male island with Chase?"

"Shut up, Dooley," said Max. "Just when we've managed to convince everyone we're females."

Dooley didn't get the joke at first, but when he did, he laughed heartily.

The van took them to the airport, where they were scheduled to take another flight, which would take them to the island in a little over an hour. And as they sat a little nervously, the van navigating the distance from the hotel to the airport, silence reigned supreme. Odelia decided to break the ice. "So how much fun is this, huh?" she said.

In response, only Tina managed to crack a feeble smile.

Kimmy decided to join Odelia's efforts to lighten the mood, and said, "How are you guys doing? Are you excited?"

Nods and murmured words of assent were her response.

"You're going to love the resort we've booked," Kimmy said. "The accommodations are amazing. This year they've added a jacuzzi, and the pool is to die for. And of course there's the bar..." She wiggled her eyebrows meaningfully.

"Oh, yeah," said the tan blonde, whose name, Odelia had learned, was Jackie. "I could murder for a gin and tonic right now."

"I could use a drink myself, to be honest," said Tina, surprising Odelia.

"I'll settle for a rum and coke," said Joanna with a nervous titter.

All eyes turned to Odelia. "What's your poison, Odelia?" asked Jackie.

"Um..." She couldn't very well confess that she wasn't much of a drinker. So instead she said, "Tequila. Always hits the spot."

Cheers rang out. Subdued, still, but a sign of things to come.

"This is going to be one big party!" Jackie cried.

*I*f I thought traveling from New York to Bangkok had been tough, the small plane we were on now was ten times worse. It shook and trembled and kept going up and down and left and right for some reason, and all the while I thought this was it—the end was nigh!

"I think I'm going to be sick," Dooley intimated from his cage, which was located right next to mine at Odelia's feet.

"Me too, buddy," I said, as I retched slightly. All this traveling was well and good, but it wasn't doing a lot for my equanimity.

"This isn't the life for me," Dooley added with a groan. "I'm a homebody, Max, not Indiana Jones or Lara Croft. Maybe Odelia should consider getting a dog and bringing *him* on her travels halfway across the world."

He was right. Travel simply does not agree with us. Still, as far as I could ascertain, we were almost there, and not a minute too soon.

"Next time I'm not coming," Dooley continued his lament. "She can bring Harriet and Brutus. They would have loved it."

"Not Brutus," I corrected him. "I think he was more than happy to be left behind. It's Harriet who's the eager one. She loves this Passion Island business and would like nothing more than to be part of the show."

"Well, she can have her show," said Dooley, in a rare case of moodiness and rebellion.

"We're almost there," I assured him. "And I'm sure once we arrive at destination's end, things will greatly improve. Exclusive five-star beach resort and all of that stuff."

"You're forgetting one thing, Max."

"What?"

"This is only the first part of the trip. We still have to get home again, which means another trip by plane, plane and plane."

And then he really did retch, depositing a nice little puddle of puke right in front of his cage. And since seeing puke always makes me want to puke, too, I quickly followed suit and deposited my neat little puddle right next to his.

"Oh, dear," said Odelia as she saw the result of our mastication on the floor. She gave us a look of commiseration. "You're really not well, are you, fellas?"

"Not well," Dooley said in shaky tones.

"Not well at all," I echoed, equally shaky. My limbs were quaking, and my stomach was twitching.

"I think I'm going to die, Odelia," said Dooley. "Please take my body back to the States and bury me in the garden underneath the rose bushes."

"Yeah, don't give us one of those burials at sea," I pleaded. "I wouldn't like to be dumped into the seething seas tucked into a plastic bag."

"I don't want to be tucked into a plastic bag and chucked into the sea either!" Dooley cried.

Odelia smiled. "You're not going to die. You're a little sick right now, but as soon as we land you'll feel right as rain again."

"You're simply saying that so we won't worry," I said.

"Yeah, you're simply saying that so we won't complain when they shove us into a plastic bag and chuck us into the sea!" Dooley cried.

"I probably should have given you something against motion sickness," said Odelia.

Behind her, suddenly a voice spoke. "Are you actually talking to your cats?" The voice was laced with a healthy dose of irony, but still Odelia sat up with a start.

"They're not feeling well," she explained to the woman. She was blond and tan and giving both me and Dooley a hard look. "Cats don't take well to travel."

"You should have gotten a dog," said the woman as she gave us a supercilious look. "Dogs are a lot more fun than cats. Cats are stupid, spiteful creatures. My mom had a cat. It scratched me so hard on my butt once you can still see the scar." And to prove she wasn't lying, she showed her left buttock, where indeed a tiny scar was visible. I wondered what she must have done to provoke such an attack in that particular place. Probably she'd taken a seat on her mother's cat by accident, at which point the creature quite naturally returned the favor by digging its claws into her behind.

Odelia clenched her jaw. She hates it when people talk smack about her cats. She refrained from lashing out, though, mostly because she was on assignment, and the first rule for an investigative reporter undercover on a case: don't antagonize your potential sources of information.

"So how did you end up joining this madhouse?" asked the woman.

"My boyfriend and I are getting married in a couple of months, and we decided to test our relationship before taking the plunge," Odelia explained. "How about you, Jackie?"

Jackie shrugged, and checked her overly long fingernails. "Money, of course. If we win this thing we'll have a nice little nest egg."

"Or a down payment to buy your own place," Odelia suggested.

Jackie laughed. "Don't you worry. We got that covered. Gary owns his own construction company. The first thing he did when we started going out was select a nice plot of land and show it to me. That's when I knew he was the one. Finally a guy who's got his priorities straight. He's already laid the foundations, and by the time we walk down the aisle our dream house will be ready for us to move in."

"Well, I'd say I hope you win, but since I hope to win myself..."

"I've seen the competition and frankly I don't think you stand a chance, sweetheart," said Jackie with a shrug. "That boyfriend of yours, and the others? They're all going down."

"And what makes you think Gary will be immune to the charms of those seductresses?"

"Because if he cheats on me, I'll kill him," said the woman, and gave Odelia a fine smile.

Next to me, Dooley gulped, and this time it wasn't from the motion of the plane. Jackie clearly was a force to be reckoned with, and I wasn't entirely sure I liked her.

$\mathcal{T}$he lodgings at the Cha Cha Resort & Residences were excellent. As Odelia inspected the little villa she'd been awarded, it was obvious the production company had spared no expense to make the candidates feel at home. The chalet was airy and bright, with a spacious bedroom and bathroom, and a salon where she could play hostess to the other candidates or... one of the seducers—or all of the above, if it pleased her.

She had absolutely no intention of doing any such thing, but she still played the game. So when Clint himself dropped by for a visit, and asked her if everything was to her satisfaction, she giggled and asked when she'd be introduced to the six seducers.

Clint grinned and said, "Now that's the spirit, young lady. You'll get to meet our seducers tonight for the first time, and rest assured you will not be disappointed."

"Thanks, Mr. Bunda," she said demurely, as befitting the profile Kimmy had drawn up for her: the not-too-clever innocent young woman, eager to expand her horizons.

"Just call me Clint," said the producer with a lascivious

twinkle in his eye. Odelia had the impression he wouldn't mind playing the seducer himself, if given the chance. "So let's go over those rules again," he said, turning serious. "No cell phones, no contact whatsoever with the other island, and participation in all the group activities as well as the dates we set up for you. Whatever you do in the privacy of your own villa, of course, is entirely up to you." He gave her a wink. "Though we will be watching."

She glanced around the spacious living area. "You have cameras in here, too?"

"Honey, we have cameras everywhere, but don't let that bother you. In fact pretend they're not even there. We always edit out the stuff that would be too embarrassing, so you just go ahead and have fun—and let us create a great show for the people back home."

And with these words, he left her to unpack.

"What a circus," said Max as he padded in from the bedroom. "And where are those cameras? I don't see them."

"That's the whole idea," said Odelia. "To make the contestants forget about them, and make absolute fools of themselves so 'the people back home' can have their voyeuristic fun." She darted a glance in the direction of the bathroom. "I wonder if they put cameras in the bathroom, too."

"Probably," said Max. "So you better shower in your bathing suit from now on. Unless you want the world to see you in your birthday suit."

"Oh, heck," said Odelia. "I'm starting to wonder why I ever said yes to this thing."

"Do you think there are bugs in here?" asked Dooley, also joining them. He'd subjected the villa to a thorough inspection, and came to deliver his field report.

"Oh, yes," said Max. "Plenty of bugs, and not the tiny, benign ones either. I think we can expect a veritable plethora of fauna and flora from now on."

Dooley shivered. "I don't like bugs, Max. They scare me. Especially the poisonous ones."

"Don't worry, buddy. I'm pretty sure there's plenty of bug spray lying around. They wouldn't want their contestants to get eaten alive before they have the chance to be seduced by one of the bigger bugs called seducers."

Odelia laughed. "I'm glad they let me bring you guys along," she said. "I would have felt pretty lonely without my two babes."

"I wonder what Harriet and Brutus are up to right now," said Dooley as he hopped up onto the couch and made himself comfortable. "Harriet really wanted to come."

"She'll be fine," Max assured him. "She'll be able to watch the show from the comfort and safety of her own home while we brave the elements to create the show."

"I hope those cameras aren't equipped with sound," Dooley said after a pause, as he darted anxious glances around the room. "Otherwise they'll wonder why one of the contestants keeps talking to her cats."

Odelia gave him a startled look. "You're right," she said. "We better watch out what we say."

"Isn't there somewhere we can speak freely?" asked Max. "A place where they haven't installed cameras?"

"There is a place," said Odelia. "Kimmy told me there's some sort of shack where the gardeners store their gear. She assured me it hasn't been wired."

"So let's meet there when we have something important to share," Max suggested.

Odelia nodded. It was also where Kimmy had told her she could safely talk to Chase. Every morning at dawn she and Chase had arranged to touch base and go over the events of the day. She was already looking forward to it. The only problem was that the rest of the resort was being watched, so she'd have to tread carefully in order to get to the shack and back without creating suspicion.

Just then, Kimmy entered and gave her a bracing smile. "How are you holding up?" she asked.

Odelia glanced around. "I feel as if I've entered a maximum-security prison."

Kimmy's smile widened. "It'll be fine," she said. "Try to relax and have some fun. Most candidates who join Passion Island have a great time on the island." Then, as she lowered her voice to a whisper, she added, "And keep your eyes peeled at all times."

And with this admonition, the young assistant producer left the villa.

17

*T*he villa where we'd arrived, our new home away from home, was very nice. It wasn't actually home, of course. And soon I started feeling a little anxious. It took Dooley to make me realize why that was.

"I miss our friends, Max," he said as we traversed the path that led from Odelia's villa to the main compound. "I miss Harriet and Brutus and Kingman and Shanille and I even miss Clarice."

"I miss them too," I told him. Then again, we'd agreed to come on this trip with Odelia, and it was important we made the best of it.

The heart of the resort consisted of a five-star restaurant where the candidates ate, a plaza with a bar, a spa, a swimming pool and second restaurant for the production crew, which ate their meals separately from the contestants. The plaza was the hub of the resort nightlife, where the seducers worked their magic to accomplish their mission.

Past the compound a path led down to the beach, and that's where we found Odelia, seated on a flat rock, gazing out across the sea at the setting sun. It was a beautiful scene, and as Dooley and I admired the picture-postcard setting, suddenly a sound like a buffalo stomping reached our ears, and as we both jerked up in anxious anticipation, a heavyset man came crashing through the brush. He sported a wispy beard, sunglasses perched on his nose, camera hoisted on his shoulder, and was dressed in a loud flowery shirt and mauve boxers. "Hey, Odelia," he said, panting. "Stay right where you are!"

Odelia, who was as startled as we were by this interruption, blinked a couple times.

"Just act as if I'm not here!" said the cameraman, which was a little hard to accomplish. "Beautiful," he murmured as he trained his camera on Odelia. "Wonderful. Amazing. Now toss your hair across your shoulders, honey. Yeah, that's it. That's the ticket, sweetie. Now give me one of those sultry looks… Love the blush! Great look."

It wasn't a blush, exactly, but more a sign of impending doom. Doom for the cameraman, though he didn't know it yet.

"Could you lose the top, sweetheart?"

Odelia gritted her teeth then snapped, "What do you think you're doing?!"

"Um… my job?" said the guy, surprised by this retort.

"Let's make one thing perfectly clear," said Odelia. "I'm not losing my top, and I'm not going to try and look sexy for your damn camera. I'm not a pinup, so get lost."

"But—"

"Get lost!"

With a sheepish look on his face, the cameraman heeded her words and got lost.

"What's a pinup, Max?" asked Dooley. "And why did that man want Odelia to get undressed?"

"I wouldn't worry too much about that, Dooley," I said. "The man was confused."

"You mean he mistook Odelia for someone else?"

"Exactly," I said. "He probably thought Odelia was his girlfriend and wanted her to pose for him."

"What a strange man," said Dooley, "that he doesn't even remember what his own girlfriend looks like."

"Some men are like that," I said. "They forget what their girlfriend looks like and start hitting on some other girl. It happens all the time." Especially on Passion Island, I could have added, but didn't. I was starting to see that this trip wasn't just dangerous for Odelia's well-being, but for Dooley's innocence, too, and was going to prove a challenge for my capacity to keep explaining away the strange happenings that took place there.

I thought it better to leave Odelia to enjoy these precious few moments of peace and quiet, so Dooley and I continued our perambulation. There were more villas spread out across the resort, not just for the contestants but also, I imagined, for the seducers, which was probably convenient. That way they could sneak into a contestant's chalet and be home before sunup. The production crew, meanwhile, stayed at a large villa on the other side of the resort, and since we weren't there to admire the view but to solve the mystery of the vanishing candidates, we decided to head on over and stake out the place.

The villa was built in hacienda style, with a wraparound porch and brightly colored window shutters. We entered the house via the front door, which was open, and found that the place was buzzing with activity. I saw the camera guy who'd accosted Odelia lament his fate to his comrades in a room off the main lobby, and watched as Clint Bunda stalked across the floor, barking orders into his cell phone. At least he was allowed to keep his phone, which didn't seem entirely fair, I thought.

I even saw Kimmy, seated in an adjacent room at a desk, bent over her laptop and typing away.

"So many people," said Dooley as we sat in a quiet corner and surveyed the activity.

"It takes a lot of people to create a big show like this," I said. "People you don't see since they all work behind the scenes."

"So how are we going to find out who's making these women disappear?" he asked.

It was an excellent question. There were easily dozens of people, holed up in the different rooms that made up the ground floor, which had been turned into offices. The room where Kimmy sat working, surrounded by others also pecking away on their laptops, had a sign that indicated this was normally the luggage room. And the room where the camera crew sat reposing was the massage parlor, though of massage activities there was to date no trace.

"Let's take a closer look," I suggested, and we moved into the room where the camera people were all gathered. The one who'd approached Odelia was still talking, and he didn't have a lot of complimentary things to say about our beloved human.

"She told me to get lost—can you believe it? I was just doing my job and she told me off! The nerve of the woman."

"Pretty little blonde, though, isn't she, our Miss Poole?" said another guy of similar dimensions, who sat fiddling with his camera. "By far the prettiest of this new crop."

"Then you haven't seen Jackie," said a third. "Just what the doctor ordered. Oo-wee!"

Somehow I had the feeling I wasn't going to learn much from listening to these men commenting on Odelia and the other women like bumblebees on a meadow of particularly nectar-filled flowers, so I told Dooley I'd heard enough and we walked out.

"They do seem to like Odelia a lot, don't they?" Dooley said.

"Yeah, I guess they do," I agreed, though I wasn't particularly partial to the kind of men who salivated over my human like a restaurant visitor over a juicy piece of steak.

We moved into the next room, but there wasn't much information to be gleaned there either. Kimmy, along with a horde of writers and fellow assistant producers, kept pecking away at their laptops in utmost concentration, so that was a bust, too.

"Let's go upstairs," I suggested. "Maybe we'll get lucky and learn something."

We moved up the stairs and arrived on the landing, several doors leading off into the crew members' respective rooms. The door to one room was ajar, and since I heard voices from inside, I decided to investigate further. No one ever pays attention to cats, which is why our association with Odelia has been so successful. We're the perfect spies.

Inside the room we found Clint, seated on the bed and still talking a mile a minute into his phone. So we took a seat near the door and listened to what he had to say.

"I don't care, Susan! It's my way or the highway, haven't I made that perfectly clear?" He listened for a moment, and I could hear a woman's voice holding up her end of the conversation. "Look, I don't want to talk about it. Because I don't want to talk about it!"

There was more repartee, and I could see that Clint was getting more and more red in the face as the conversation dragged on.

"I think he's going to have an aneurysm, Max," said Dooley, noticing the same thing.

"I think so, too," I agreed, and was already eyeing the door in case we needed to race out to fetch Odelia and a doctor.

"Look, it's got nothing to do with me. If they decide to

vanish from the face of the earth that's their business. How the hell would I know where they've gone off to! It's got nothing to do with me, I'm telling you!"

I had the impression he was talking about the missing women, so I pricked up my ears. Unfortunately, the conversation quickly wound down after that, and so before Clint discovered he was no longer alone, Dooley and I tip-toed from the room again.

Out in the corridor, Dooley said, "I think he was talking about the missing women, Max."

"I think you're right."

"Does that mean he doesn't know where they are?"

"I'm not sure," I said. "But I think we can put Clint's name on our list of suspects."

Though why the show's producer would kidnap his own contestants was beyond me.

18

That night, the first big event of the season had been announced and was to take place in the plaza, the central meeting place, and not coincidentally where the bar was located. Before Odelia had left for Thailand she'd watched a couple of episodes of the show's previous season, conveniently taped by her grandmother, and it struck her that a lot of the 'action' appeared to take place in that very same plaza.

So it was with a slight sense of trepidation that she slid into the little black dress she'd selected for the occasion, slipped her feet into a pair of heels, and checked her reflection in the mirror. She'd applied minimal makeup, and her hair was a little frizzy, but she figured she'd be able to get away with it. After all, she hadn't been cast as a seductress but as one half of a regular couple, and she looked about as regular as could be.

As she left the villa, she almost bumped into Tina, who was dressed to the nines, and looked absolutely terrified. "I've already downed two martinis and I still feel like I'm going to die," the homely brunette confessed.

"It'll be fine," Odelia said, though she felt seriously nervous herself.

"It's not the seducers I'm worried about so much as all those cameras. And the idea that millions of people will be watching my every move, and listening to every single thing I say. Can you believe a guy with a camera came into my bedroom just now, filming me? I kicked him out, of course." She shook her head. "The gall of these people. Just because we signed up for their show they think they can do anything."

"I had to get rid of a cameraman myself," Odelia said. "Kept bugging me about removing my top."

"We're candidates, not strippers," said Tina as she teetered on her high heels.

They passed a villa and a loud voice arrested their progress. "Hey, wait up!" The voice belonged to Jackie, and she looked absolutely gorgeous in a skintight red dress that showcased a sizable bust and a pair of long tan legs. She came tripping up, a look of excitement on her face. "I can't believe the show is about to start and we're in it!" she cried. "Isn't that just amazeballs! Eeeek!"

"Eeeek!" Tina echoed, though it was clear her heart wasn't really in it.

"Eeeeek!" said Odelia without much enthusiasm.

The fourth participant came walking out of her villa and smiled when she saw the three others waiting for her on the path.

"So this is it, huh?" she said. Joanna was dressed in a simple white linen dress, and looked the most normal of the foursome. Like Odelia, she hadn't put on a lot of makeup, and it was obvious the pretty redhead wasn't exactly the party girl. She heaved a little sigh. "Is it just me or do you guys just want this whole thing to be over?"

"It's just you!" said Jackie, and squealed again. And as she slipped her arm through Tina's, and started up the path, Odelia and Joanna fell back.

"You don't seem like the Passion Island type either," said Joanna. "Are you sure you're in the right place?" She laughed deferentially. "I know I've had my doubts myself."

Odelia experienced a pang of guilt for lying to these women. Still, she had to stick to her story. She couldn't very well come out and tell Joanna she was there in an official capacity. "I don't really care about the whole show element either," she confessed, "but the prize money could really change my life. In my line of work 50.000 dollars is a lot of money. I'd have to work my whole life to raise that kind of cash."

"What do you do for a living?"

"I'm a reporter for a small-town newspaper on Long Island. Lots of local events. You know the kind. Wedding anniversaries, library readings, a farmer's chickens organizing the great escape. Not exactly Pulitzer-Prize-winning material. I love it, though."

"I thought you were a vet or something," said Joanna. "Because of the cats."

"Oh, no. Though it's true that I love my two fur-babies."

"They are pretty cute," said Joanna with a smile.

"How about you? What do you do?"

"I'm an accountant, and so is my Arthur. In fact that's how we met. My parents are accountants, too. They run their own company, and Arthur was their first hire, so we ended up spending a lot of time together crunching numbers, and chatting around the water cooler. And one thing led to another and here we are." She smiled. "Friends signed us up for Passion Island. They figured we could use a little excitement in our lives."

"Oh, they did, did they?"

"Why is it that people always think accountants are boring?" asked Joanna, a tiny frown slicing her brow.

"I have absolutely no idea," Odelia said with a smile. She liked Joanna. She was nice. "So do you think Arthur will be able to resist the charms of those seductresses?"

"Oh, sure. Arthur adores me. He told me we'd easily win this thing."

They'd arrived at the plaza, and were greeted by a camera crew, bright lights competing with the natural light still being dispensed by a sun slowly sinking behind the horizon.

"Welcome, ladies!" Clint said, a toothy grin on his face. "Let me introduce you to your host: Francine Richter!"

Gasps of excited anticipation escaped four throats, even Odelia's. Francine Richter, the famous show host, looked absolutely gorgeous. She was pushing fifty, but didn't look a day over thirty-five. Not a hair of her platinum coiffure was out of place, her slender frame clad in a bright yellow dress was stunning, and her famous features were arranged in an appropriately welcoming smile.

"Hello, ladies," she said in that deep voice instantly recognizable to viewers around the country. "So how are you feeling today? Are you excited to be part of Passion Island?"

"You bet!" Jackie cried, and the other three women all concurred, though in slightly less exuberant tones, due to being awestruck by the presence of network royalty.

And as Clint melted into the background, Francine expertly took control of the interview. For a couple of minutes she chatted easily and brightly with the four contestants, eliciting a few sound bites about their background and motivation to be on the show, and then it was time for the moment they'd all been waiting for: the introduction of the seducers.

Odelia swallowed. She wasn't there for the show, really, but she still couldn't help but be swept up in the excitement of the moment. She'd never been on TV before, and certainly never on a popular reality show.

Then, as music blasted from the speakers, lights flashed, and the smoke machine worked overtime, six men came strutting onto the dance floor and performed an exhilarating dance routine. They looked like the lineup of a Chippendales show, or that movie with Channing Tatum: steely-eyed looks, chiseled faces, granite jaw lines, gleaming rock-hard pecs, and bulging muscles, these men took their fitness routines seriously!

"Oh, my," Joanna said next to Odelia, as a gasp escaped Tina, and Jackie screamed her head off with excitement.

19

"*M*ax?"

"Mh?"

"Why are those men so shiny?"

"Oil," I said curtly. I would have said more, but just like everyone present I was transfixed by the strange spectacle of six grown men gyrating not twenty feet from where I was sitting, dressed like Tarzan and throwing glances that can only be described as lascivious at the four young ladies for whom this spectacle was clearly intended.

"Oil?"

"Oil."

"But why, Max? Why are they dressed in oil and not much else?"

"I think their costume—or lack thereof—is designed to impress, Dooley." And judging from the rapturous expressions on the faces of their audience it was clear their very particular dress code had hit its mark. Even Odelia looked as if she'd bitten down on a delicious piece of yummy chocolate and the taste had exploded across her palate.

"Why is Odelia's mouth hanging open, Max?" Dooley continued his barrage of tough questions.

His powers of observation were excellent, though. In fact he was probably understating things, as our human's jaw was practically on the floor now.

"She's probably hot," I said. It was pretty hot out, even though the sun was setting.

"I don't think Chase is going to like this," said Dooley. "I don't think he's going to like it that she's looking at those men like that."

"Oh, I don't know," I said. "She's probably surprised, that's all." After all, it isn't every day that all of a sudden, and quite out of the blue, six grown men of the Adonis type are suddenly performing a routine that's usually reserved for the kind of clubs I'm sure Odelia doesn't lend her patronage. "Besides," I added. "It's not as if Chase can see her. He's on a completely different island, with no way of knowing what his fiancée is up to."

Then my eyes shifted to the row of cameras filming every single moment of the sordid little scene and I gulped a little. Oops.

❧

One island over, Chase Kingsley was not having a good time. If he'd hoped going undercover in the belly of the Passion Island beast would give him a wealth of clues as to the dark underpinnings of the reality show, and lead him to unmask the evil conspiracy at its heart, that hope had yet to be borne out.

So far all he'd done was chat with three rather obnoxious young men, whose only intention apparently was to have fun with as many women as possible before tying the knot with their ones and only, and watch those same men down copious amounts of alcohol to 'get in the mood.'

He hoped Odelia was having better luck, because as far as he was concerned this operation so far was a bust.

He was seated at the bar, waiting for the moment of the big reveal—the introduction of the six seductresses, whose unenviable task it was to break up four happy couples.

It all sounded pretty immoral as far as Chase was concerned, and his low opinion of the show's producer, Clint Bunda, was hitting new lows as he listened to the boasts and brags of his three co-contestants.

To Chase, relationships were a sacred bond between a man and a woman, and these Passion Island shenanigans were seriously getting on his nerves. To the extent he'd had to suppress a powerful urge to put these men in their place for being so cavalier.

"It's happening!" suddenly declared Nick, a stringy young man whose hair hadn't survived an attack of attrition. His betrothed was a girl named Tina, and according to his drunken braggadocio they'd made a secret arrangement that he could bed any seductress he wanted, as a way of sowing his wild oats one last time before entering a state of wedded bliss.

Chase had his doubts about this so-called arrangement, but hadn't given vent to his skepticism. He didn't want to blow his cover by going overboard on the heavy-handedness. He was, after all, one of the boys, though right now he felt more like an adult surrounded by a couple of rambunctious teenagers.

On the dance floor, the spotlights were showing off their stroboscopic prowess as four ladies sashayed onto the scene, all dressed in tiny thongs and even tinier string bikinis. All four were extremely tan, thin and showcasing the kind of physique only attainable with the assistance of a skilled plastic surgeon, personal trainer and stylist. To Chase's dismay, they reminded him of life-sized Barbie dolls. Not exactly his dream dates, though judging from the uproarious grunts and howls from his co-islanders, they couldn't have disagreed more.

And as they produced the kind of animal sounds befitting this jungle environment, the lanky cop expelled a tired groan.

"Hey, why are there only four?" asked Arthur suddenly.

Chase narrowed his eyes. The accountant was right. Six seductresses had been advertised, but only four were stalking across the platform.

"Oh, there they are," said Nick.

And, much to Chase's surprise, suddenly two more seductresses materialized—and they looked very familiar indeed.

"What the…" one of the men muttered.

Four jaws drooped, Chase's included, as two mature ladies appeared. One was dressed in a pink tracksuit, and the other in a tiger-print catsuit.

They were Grandma Muffin and Scarlett Canyon.

20

"*I* think we're on the wrong island, sweetums."

"Shush, Brutus," said Harriet.

"No, but I mean it. We're on the men's island. We were supposed to be on the women's island."

"It doesn't matter!"

"But it does, sugar plum. The women's island is where it's at. That's where the investigation is taking place."

"I'm going to be on camera whether they like it or not," said Harriet, clearly not paying attention to a word her mate had said.

She had that resolute look in her eyes that Brutus knew all too well. It often spelled trouble, and already he was trying to anticipate Harriet's next move so he could talk her out of it, but this time she was too quick, even for one as closely familiar with her wiles as he was.

Before he could stop her, she was already stalking off in the direction of the plaza.

"Harriet!" he called out, but the music pounding from the speakers was so loud even her fine feline sense of hearing couldn't have picked up his cry of despair.

He watched helplessly as Harriet joined the lineup of six women and started a series of gyrations that could easily compete with those of the dancing Barbies.

Brutus shook his head in frustration. He knew how keen Harriet was to be part of Passion Island, but this was too much. If she kept this up she'd be booted off the island!

The men seated at the bar were all whooping and hollering, except Chase, who looked a little green around the gills.

It's one thing to have to watch four would-be strippers, but another to see your future grandmother-in-law strutting her stuff like a seasoned Jezebel, along with her newly-found best friend, a seventy-year-old woman having squeezed her pneumatic frame into a much-too-tight leopard-skin excuse for a garment.

The four other women kept darting curious glances at Scarlett, probably wondering if that's what they'd look like in another forty or fifty years, but Scarlett didn't appear bothered. Quite the opposite. While the other women strutted their stuff in situ, she decided to venture out into the world and now approached the candidates, quickly curling herself around a large and portly one, much to the latter's obvious delight.

Scarlett Canyon might have celebrated her seventh decade on this planet, but with all the work she'd had done she easily looked decades younger. And of course the men had been drinking steadily all evening, and the booze must have affected their eyesight.

Brutus eyed the spectacle of four Barbie wannabes, one Persian cat and one septuagenarian dressed like Estelle Getty with a jaundiced eye.

Things could only get better from this point onward. Couldn't they?

"*W*hat do you think you're doing?" Chase hissed.

"Oh, come off your high horse, Mr. Cop," said Gran, waving away his objections. "Now what does a girl have to do to get a drink around here? Preferably one of them umbrella ones."

They were seated at the bar, the show having ended when one of the producers had pulled the plug on the sound system and ordered the cameras to stop rolling. He'd looked on the verge of having a heart attack and had screamed something that sounded a lot like 'Get rid of that darn cat!'

"You're not seriously considering sticking around, are you?" Chase asked, incredulous.

"Of course I'm sticking around! I didn't come all this way to get kicked off this island so soon." She tilted her chin. "I have every right to be here, same as you."

Chase couldn't believe his ears. "But you're a cheat!"

Gran had heard through the grapevine that two of the seductresses had had to drop out at the last minute and had sent in her and Scarlett's applications to be their replacements. Only they hadn't mentioned their ages, and they'd used pictures from a stock photo website. And since time was of the essence, they'd been quickly sent the go-ahead. Only when they'd suddenly appeared in the lineup had the production team realized that the two ladies they'd figured were part of the kitchen staff were in fact their much-sought-after new replacement seductresses.

"Look, I told that idiot that if he dares kick us off the island I'm going to sue him for ageism. It's time that senior citizens get their due. It's not fair that only the young get to have fun. He quickly backed down after that." She smacked her lips as she bellowed, "Waiter! One of 'em umbrella drinks for me! Yeah, the fruity ones!"

"You're going to ruin this whole operation," Chase said, as he rubbed his face.

"Nothing of the kind. I'm going to *save* your operation. You didn't think this through, Chase. You and Odelia infiltrated the show as fake candidates—"

"Not so loud!" Chase hissed.

"But who's infiltrating the seductresses, huh?" She thumped her chest. "Me!"

"Oh, God…" Chase muttered.

"You didn't think, sonny boy! Where do you think the danger is coming from? Exactly those wily seductresses. They're the ones setting up this whole kidnapping scheme. Listen, I've got it all figured out. The seductresses seduce the men, right?"

"Mh."

"And of course they want to keep them once the show is over, cause these are some pretty fine specimens. Not the kind of guys who normally go for the stripper type, right?"

"Are you going somewhere with this?"

"Just listen! So once the show is over, and the cameras are gone, and the free booze, and the sun and the beach and the rest, these men of course land back in reality with a thud. Back to work on Monday. Back to their regular lives, with their regular fiancées."

"If they'll still have them," Chase muttered.

"Of course they will. This is just one long stag party. But these women don't want it to be over. They want to hook these men once and for all. So how to work it? By getting rid of the competition. They whack the future wives, step into their roles and bingo! A great life awaits. With a pretty boring husband, granted, but that's why adultery was invented."

"You're forgetting one thing."

"I doubt it."

"The women are on the other island."

"So? They don't get abducted straightaway, do they? These women must have accomplices waiting until the candidates return to the States, and nab them first chance they get. Now where's that drink? Hey, waiter! I can see what you're doing, you sneaky little twerp! You're serving the bimbos first! Wanna get sued for ageism? Cause I'll do it! Thanks," she added, and took a satisfied sip from her umbrella drink. "Aaah," she said, closing her eyes. "Now that hits the spot."

21

That night, a first campfire was being held on both islands. As Kimmy had explained, the campfire was when the candidates were all gathered around a fire and shown footage of what their other halves were up to on the other island. It was usually a moment fraught with a certain measure of dread, as Clint liked to throw in a couple of grenades in the form of infidelities engaged in by the candidates and watch the fallout.

Odelia, as she took a seat, glanced at her fellow candidates. Jackie looked extremely jolly, as her blood was now presumably one hundred percent pure alcohol after having knocked back more G&T's than probably was good for her. Tina was chewing her bottom lip, looking anxious, and Joanna was yawning, indicating it was way past her bedtime.

After the show had wound down, the six Chippendale wannabes had mingled with the contestants at the bar, and immediately one of them had hit on Odelia. She'd made it clear from the outset that she wasn't interested, though, earning her a wounded look from the male model. The moment he'd vacated his seat another one had taken his place, and this one hadn't taken no for an answer, and had spent the rest of the evening trying to break down her defenses, which of course was what he was being paid to do.

He wasn't an unpleasant guy, though, so she'd endured his company, but had steered the conversation resolutely away from the more romantic topics.

Jackie, meanwhile, hadn't been as reticent as Odelia, and had stuck so close to two of the seducers she could have described their physique with her eyes closed. Tina and Joanna had also spent the evening being wooed, though Odelia doubted with much luck.

Francine Richter joined them at the campfire, which was actually a black metal terrace heater. She was clutching an iPad, a look of significance in her eyes.

For Passion Island aficionados this was the highlight of the show.

"So this is it, ladies," said the show host. "Are you ready for the moment of truth?"

"Please tell me nothing happened," said Tina, having transferred her chewing activities from her lip to her fingernails.

"You'll soon find out," said Francine ominously, and swiped the iPad with a long-nailed finger.

The screen flickered to life and footage of a similar nature to what had happened on Koh Samui appeared: over on Koh Phangan the four candidates were seated at the bar, Chase amongst them, and then the seductresses arrived and the party started.

Odelia's shocked gasp echoed the gasps of the other three contestants when Gran and Scarlett suddenly appeared in the lineup!

"What's this?" asked Jackie. "Is this a joke?"

"Um, in the spirit of diversification we've decided to

allow women of all ages to compete for the candidates' attention," Francine said, clearly lying through her teeth.

Odelia had no idea how Gran had pulled this off, but obviously she had!

"Nick likes older women," Tina said miserably. "In fact he loves them."

Odelia doubted whether even Nick would fall for the charms of Gran or Scarlett, but she rubbed Tina's back consolingly. The latter gave her a watery smile in return, then fixed her eyes on the screen again for signs of her future husband's infidelity.

"What's that cat doing there?" asked Joanna.

And she was right: a cat was prancing around in front of the line of seductresses. And it was a cat Odelia knew all too well. It was Harriet!

"Passion Island is really going down," said Jackie a little angrily. "First those two old biddies and now a cat. If I'd known…"

Her words stuck in her throat as her boyfriend Gary came into view. The builder was busily examining the tonsils of one of the seductresses with his tongue, and only came up for air when the camera was so close to his face he could probably feel the static electricity.

"Bastard!" Jackie cried. "The cheating bastard!"

Her fiancé had the gall to grin at the camera like a boy caught with his fingers in the cookie jar, then simply picked up where he left off and went right back to his deep space exploration.

"I'll get him for this," Jackie growled, balling her fists. "I'll teach him a lesson he'll never forget!"

"Strictly speaking he hasn't cheated on you, Jackie," Francine said. "We don't count kissing as cheating, remember. Only when we catch a candidate in bed with a seducer do we strike the gong."

BOOOOING!

Suddenly the sound of a gong reverberated through the resort. Someone had been caught cheating, and judging from the pitch, it was one of the male contestants.

"Oh, he's done it now," said Jackie, getting up. Then she screamed at the top of her lungs, "I'll get you for this, Gary Goulash!"

She stomped off in the direction of the plaza, presumably to drown her sorrow.

"It could be anyone," said Joanna. "It could be my Arthur."

"We'll find out tomorrow," Francine assured them. "At the next campfire."

Which meant that all day tomorrow Joanna, Tina and Odelia would be held in suspense, not knowing whether their significant other had been unfaithful or not.

Though Odelia was pretty sure it couldn't have been Chase. He wasn't that kind of guy.

Or was he?

Spend long enough on Passion Island and anything could happen...

22

The sound of the gong had also had a powerful effect on the other side of the stretch of water. The male contestants were all gathered around a similar campfire, only no Francine Richter was in evidence but George Foulard.

Like Miss Richter, Mr. Foulard was a veteran broadcaster, with a long pedigree as a show host. His gray hair gave him that respectful look, but it didn't fool Chase. The man was as cunning and clever as they came, and as George looked up when the gong was struck, his eyes glistened mischievously.

"Oops," he said. "Now who could that possibly be?"

It wasn't hard to guess, as only one man had failed to show up for their campfire tryst, that man being Gary Goulash. As Gary had been playing tonsil hockey with one of the seductresses all evening, he probably felt it incumbent upon him to carry on his efforts in the privacy of his own bedroom, where Clint's cameras had caught him in flagrante delicto, hence the sound of the gong.

It made for a welcome change, as the campfire hadn't supplied its promised excitement: even though the women had engaged with the seducers, and had stood them a couple for drinks, no improprieties had ensued, and even Jackie, who'd seemed like the type of girl to whom fidelity was an elastic concept, had merely danced with but not kissed her prince for the night.

Chase had watched with a certain measure of disquiet how Odelia had chatted with not one but two seducers, and when one of the latter had placed his hand on her arm had felt his blood go to a boil. The sudden powerful urge to wipe the man's smirk from his face by means of planting his fist in his mouth was so overpowering he was already calculating how long it would take him to swim to the other island, the talk of dangerous currents and undercurrents and even potential sharks having been wiped from his mind.

"Looks like we're the lucky ones," said Joanna's fiancé, clapping Chase on the back. "Just look at my sweet baby girl. Doesn't even flinch when that tattooed fool flexes his ridiculously pumped-up bicep in her face."

Nick, too, looked relieved. "Tina would never go for a guy like that," he said, indicating the screen. "She's more into the intellectual type, like me."

If Nick was an intellectual, Chase was RuPaul, but he merely smiled encouragingly and unflexed his fists. He wasn't fully sanguine, though. He knew Clint would do whatever it took to make the women fall for their seducers. After all, that's why Passion Island had become the network's top-rated show.

&

"So... Gran is on the other island?" asked Dooley.
"Yes. And so is Scarlett Canyon," I said. "And Harriet and Brutus."
"But... why? And how?"

"I have absolutely no idea, Dooley. But I'm sure we'll soon find out."

Odelia had slept but fitfully, tossing and turning all night. Dooley and I, ensconced at the foot of the bed, as is our habit, had watched it with a worried eye. Apart from the fact that I don't like it when Odelia moves around, afraid she'll kick me in the snoot and send me flying off the bed, I hate to see my human troubled, and troubled she clearly was.

So far she hadn't been able to chat with anyone from the production team, and it was exactly those people she needed to get close to if she was going to uncover what had happened to those other women.

Unfortunately Clint had instigated a rule that his staff refrain from getting too close to the candidates the moment the show started. In previous incarnations some of the cameramen hadn't been able to resist the temptation to schmooze with some of the seductresses, and some of them had even hooked up. So this year the staff kept to their own villa, while the contestants stayed in their own little bubble with the seducers.

Morning had finally broken, and we watched as Odelia opened first one eye then the other.

"Wakey-wakey, sleepyhead," I said.

She groaned and buried her face in her pillow. "I dreamt I was home," she muttered.

"Usually people dream of being on a tropical island, all expenses paid," I pointed out to her.

"Yeah, but those people haven't been asked to try and unmask some abductor of women," she replied, then turned and rubbed her eyes.

"I think you should really try to enjoy yourself more, Odelia," said Dooley. "Maybe forget about the investigation for a couple of days and have some fun?"

"Yeah, you could go for a swim," I suggested. "The beach

looks particularly beautiful. And I heard that today you're all going jet-skiing, so that should be a blast, right?"

Being dragged at a high rate of speed behind a boat, only two thin slices of styrofoam between you and the raging shark-infested waters of a deep sea didn't sound like something I'd enjoy, but then humans are strange creatures. Some of them even like to climb mountains, which is something I thought only a certain species of goats enjoy.

"Jet skiing," Odelia muttered as she dragged herself from the bed. "Great. Just what I need. More attempts by Mike to try and get into bed with me."

"Why does Mike want to get into your bed?" asked Dooley. "Doesn't he like his own bed?"

Odelia smiled. "I guess not," she said, then slouched out of the room and into the bathroom.

Twenty minutes later she'd put on running shoes, and was dressed in a T-shirt and running shorts and looked a lot less like something Dooley or myself had dragged in.

"Let's go, you guys," she said, performing a strange movement known as jumping jacks.

And then we were off, for our first run.

It was seven o'clock in the morning and already it was heating up quickly. And Odelia had only run five minutes before a stitch in my side halted my progress.

Cats are built for sprints, you see, not marathons.

"You go on ahead," I said as I pressed a paw to my side. "I'll get there in my own time!"

Dooley, too, was out of breath already.

And as we watched Odelia disappear around a bend in the dirt path, we both settled down in the shade of a nearby palm tree, languorously lying in the tall cool grass.

And just as I was catching my breath again, who'd pass us by but a long, thin man with a nasty scar slicing his brow and a slight limp!

23

"Let's go, Max!" Dooley cried, and was up and running before the fact that Scarface had once again entered the picture had thoroughly registered in my mind.

It's easy to say 'Let's go' when you're as lissome as Dooley, but a lot harder to accomplish when you're blessed with big bones like me. By the time I'd managed to break the hold gravity held over me and was going well, a certain amount of time had elapsed.

So for the reader of these chronicles it might be a good idea to reiterate the state of affairs: there was Odelia, running like a young foal, eager to have speech with her fiancé, then Scarface, no doubt filled with nefarious thoughts of snatching young maidens in the bloom of their lives and doing God knows what with them, then Dooley, running full out, conscious of a strong desire to protect said maiden, and finally, at a distance, your correspondent, huffing and puffing in the morning heat, and perspiring like a long-distance runner about to pass mile twenty and moving into the home stretch.

My paws were killing me, and so was my belly which, for

some inexplicable reason, kept flopping around as I pottered on. And it was as I was starting to see red spots moving into my field of vision that I caught up with Dooley, who'd caught up with Scarface, who'd caught up with Odelia, who was now glancing around furtively and entered a sad-looking little shack built next to a tall fence lining the resort's domain.

Scarface had ducked behind a bush of uncertain antecedents, and Dooley had ducked behind another bush, so as to spy on the spy. I joined my friend in his bush.

"What's going on?" I asked as I plunked down heavily. I had the feeling I was melting, as sweat dripped from my paws, the only area, I might add, cats can sweat through, and I was glad for the reprieve. Even though I dislike Vena Aleman, our designated vet, I had a feeling she would have looked at me askance right now, for exerting myself to this extent.

"Scarface is talking into his phone," said Dooley. "And Odelia just went into that shack over there."

"We should be in that shack," I said, gulping like a fish on dry land, "finding out what's going on with Chase and the others."

"But if we go into the shack we can't keep an eye on Scarface," Dooley pointed out, and I had to admit he was right.

"I think it's the heat," I said, waving a paw in front of my face. "It's starting to affect my mental faculties."

Scarface was indeed talking into his phone, then held it up in the manner perfected by all amateur smartphone users in the direction of the shack. He was clearly filming Odelia again, which seemed to be some kind of obsession with this horrible man.

"He must be the guy who keeps abducting women," I said after I'd filled my lungs with some much-needed oxygen.

"Do you think he wants to kidnap Odelia?" asked Dooley, sounding shocked.

"I think so. He broke into her room and filmed her sleeping, then tried to access her laptop and tablet computer, and now he's filming her again. The guy is obsessed with her, that much is obvious."

"We have to warn her, Max. The moment she comes out of that shack he'll grab her."

"I don't think so. He could have grabbed her before, and he didn't. He's waiting for something. Watching and waiting."

Dooley shivered. "It's very creepy."

"It is," I agreed. "Come on. Let's circle around and enter that shack from the back."

I'd recovered enough to perform this feat, and soon we found ourselves at the other side of the shack, and to our elation managed to sneak inside through a crack in the dilapidated structure's side.

"It's one theory," Odelia was saying, "though it sounds very unlikely to me, if I'm honest."

"Yeah, it sounds pretty unlikely to me, too," we heard Chase respond when Odelia put the phone in speaker mode.

"Gran thinks the seductresses are behind the kidnappings," Odelia explained for our sake. "So they can marry their husbands," she added when we stared at her, a lack of comprehension apparently written all over our features. "So how are you holding up?" Odelia asked now.

"I'm fine," said Chase. "But can I ask you a question? Who's the guy you were chatting with last night?"

Odelia smiled. "Oh, that's just Mike. He's harmless."

"Mike, huh," said Chase, and his voice betrayed his displeasure.

Odelia giggled. "You're not jealous, are you?"

"Of course I'm jealous! I have to sit here while Magic Mike tries his best moves on my girl."

"I can handle Mike, don't worry. And I have no intention of causing the gong to go off," said Odelia, sounding amused. "How about you? You were having a great time with some of those seductresses."

"If you mean your grandmother, who I spent half the night talking to at the bar, I think it's safe to say you have nothing to worry about."

"No, I don't mean my grandmother. I mean that blond bimbo who couldn't stop staring at your butt."

"Oh, Dina. She's all right. I told her I'm not interested and she accepts that. She's a Passion Island veteran. This is her third time as a seductress. So I hoped to squeeze her for information."

"Just make sure she doesn't squeeze you back."

I'd been trying to catch Odelia's attention, but she was so wrapped up in her conversation about Mike and Dina that she was steadfastly ignoring me.

"There's a guy out there spying on you!" I finally blurted out.

She frowned and looked down at me and Dooley. "What? Who?"

"Scarface," said Dooley. "He followed you from the villa and he's out there filming."

Odelia gulped a little, then glanced out through the small windows. "Are you sure? I don't—oh, crap, I see him. Chase, Scarface is back, and he's followed me down here!"

"Try to sneak out the back," was the cop's advice, "then alert security and tell them some creep has been following you around."

She disconnected and I pointed at the broken plank that had facilitated our access. She took a good grip and pulled hard. It easily broke off, and she repeated the procedure with its neighbor. Now she'd created a hole wide enough to slip through, which she did, followed by Dooley and me.

And as she crawled through the undergrowth, thoroughly ruining her nice T-shirt, I stealthily returned to see if Odelia's departure had been observed.

Scarface was still in position, though, and talking into his phone again.

I quickly made my way back to my human, and together the three of us circled around and started our way back to the compound.

The sun had crept a little higher across the horizon and the world was quickly heating up.

"Now I understand why I haven't seen a single cat on this island," I told Dooley. "It's too hot for the likes of us, what with our thick coat of fur."

"Maybe I should shave you guys?" Odelia suggested.

"Ha ha," I said. "Over my dead body."

We quickly arrived back at the site, and Odelia made a beeline for the villa that housed the staff. The first person we met was Kimmy, and Odelia quickly told the production assistant of our unfortunate encounter with Scarface.

Kimmy's face took on a grave expression. "I'll tell security. Hopefully they can still catch the guy."

And as Dooley and I watched on, the villa came to life: beefy security men came hurrying out, then hopped into a jeep, and soon were off, after having received instructions from Odelia, detailing Scarface's last known location.

"I hope they catch him," said Dooley.

"Yeah, I hope so, too."

"Though if they do catch him, our job here is done, right? And we get to go home again?"

"I think so," I said.

He looked happy at the prospect, and I have to confess I felt happy, too. A cat is never happier than when close to home and hearth. It's strange but true. After all, we're not dogs. Dogs enjoy prancing around the world like hapless globetrotters. Us cats do not. We're homebodies, and proud to be so.

I'd only been there a day and already I missed cat choir, and my friends, and my couch, and my daily routine.

Besides, I was way too hot—and not prepared to allow Odelia to shave me. Uh-uh. No way! I prefer to suffer in silence than to end up looking like a fool. Have you ever seen a hairless cat? They're weird!

Besides, I love my blorange coat of fur. It's part of my personality. It's who I am.

So I decided to sweat, and not fret, and when ten minutes later the jeep returned, and I saw that they'd managed to capture the scar-faced man, I was over the moon.

Our adventure was over.

We were going home!

24

"*B*ut he's my gaffer!" Clint cried as he walked out of the villa to survey the scene. "What the hell do you think you're doing, spying on my contestants!" he added with a good deal of ire.

Scarface had been deposited in front of the big boss, and Odelia, having crossed her arms and eyeing the man with no small measure of pique, had been joined by pretty much the entire contingent marooned on the island, fellow candidates and seducers included.

Scarface wilted a little under the attention, and seemed genuinely unnerved, like a man dragged before the police court after having been caught driving under the influence.

"I'm... a reporter," he finally said, in a surprisingly reedy voice. "The name is Jack Davenport and I'm doing a piece on Passion Island for the National Star."

"The National Star!" Clint, cried, throwing his hands in the air. "So you mean to tell me you're not a gaffer?"

"An amateur gaffer at best," said the man, looking distinctly ill at ease.

"But why did you break into my room and film me in my sleep?" asked Odelia.

"Plenty of these so-called couples aren't couples at all," said the guy with a shrug. "So my editor told me to try and catch you in the act, meaning sleeping apart. You guys are a real couple, though," he said, offering Odelia a faint smile.

"So you spied on all of my candidates?!" thundered Clint.

"Yeah, and I gotta say all of them are for real, man."

"Of course they're for real!"

"My editor thought otherwise, so he sent me in to expose this show as a fabrication. But so far that hasn't been my experience. Everything looks above board. Not a message my editor wanted to hear, mind you. I can tell you he was pretty disappointed."

"Well, you can tell your editor he can go and boil his head!" Clint said, and stormed into the house. Then, apparently having changed his mind, he came storming out again. "On second thought, why don't you stick around?"

"Stick around?" asked Jack Davenport.

"Stick around?!" asked Odelia, aghast.

"Yeah, if you promise to give the show a good write-up, you can stick around. If not, you can go to hell."

"I'd rather stick around, sir," said Jack.

"Great. I look forward to reading your article," said Clint with a nod.

"You can't do this!" Odelia cried. "He broke into my room!"

Clint shrugged. "Nobody's perfect."

"I'm sorry, Miss Poole," said Jack later, as he and Odelia were seated at the breakfast table. "I know your work and I'm a great admirer. So when my editor told me to film all the contestants in their sleep, I balked at the idea. But he told me that if I didn't do it, he'd send someone who would. And I need the job. My wife is pregnant with our first, and I can't afford to be out of work right now. You know how hard it is to be a reporter these days. Not a lot of jobs to go around."

"I still think it's a pretty crap thing to do," said Odelia as she bit down on a chocolate croissant with cream filling. The food at the resort was amazing. If she wasn't careful she'd go home ten pounds heavier than when she set out for Thailand.

"I hope you can forgive me," said Jack.

"I actually thought you were a kidnapper."

"A kidnapper!"

"Yeah, the way you came after me this morning."

"I was just trying to get a couple of good shots for my article. And when I saw you take off running the opportunity was too good to miss." He thoughtfully took a sip from his coffee. "What were you doing in that shack if I may ask? It almost looked as if you were on the phone with someone, which of course is impossible, since candidates aren't allowed to have phones."

Odelia studied the guy. Now that he'd told them his name, she knew who he was. She'd read his articles. He was a pretty sharp observer, and a great writer. What he was doing writing for a tabloid she didn't know. Then again, as he said, it wasn't easy finding work as a reporter these days. She wondered how much to tell him, then decided to trust her gut.

"I'm not here as a candidate, Jack. I'm here as a reporter. Some of the contestants from previous editions have gone missing, and I'm trying to figure out what's going on."

Jack whistled through his teeth. "Now that's the kind of story I wouldn't mind breaking. Missing, you say? How come I haven't heard about this?"

"Because their families haven't filed missing person reports. They're still in touch with them, through email and letters and postcards. But it's too much of a coincidence that five women, all of them former contestants, would take off like that."

"Yeah, I'd say the odds of that happening are pretty slim."

"My fiancé is a cop, and he's on the other island checking things out over there, while I'm here, trying to see if I can find out what's going on."

"And you thought I was involved," said Jack, nodding.

"Can you blame me?"

He shook his head and smiled, then fingered his scar absentmindedly.

"Can I ask you a personal question?" asked Odelia.

"I fell from my bike when I was five," said Jack, anticipating. "The doctor who patched me up did a pretty lousy job and the wound got infected. I could get it fixed, but I've found that it actually helps in my line of work. The bad guys figure I'm one of them, and the good guys feel sorry and get gabby." He grinned. "So I just leave it. I call it my lucky scar, and my wife doesn't seem to mind."

"You know?" said Odelia, throwing down her napkin. "We could team up. Whatever we discover, we share the credit. What do you say?"

"Oh, I'd love nothing more," said Jack. "Spying on reality show participants isn't as exciting as it sounds."

They both laughed, and shook hands on it.

"So we're not going home?" asked Dooley sadly.

"We're not going home," I said, just as sadly.

We were both lying on the beach, watching the Passion Island contestants being dragged around the Gulf of Thailand on jet skis. And when I say we were on the beach, I mean, of course, on the edge of the beach, safely and comfortably nestled on the terrace of one of those beach restaurants that appear to infest beaches the world over, and offer refreshments, ice cream, and the opportunity for a sanitary break if so desired, though of course most beach-goers use the wide-open oceans or seas as their convenient latrine.

"Jack Davenport," said Dooley, and in his eyes was a look that said what exactly he thought of this reporter.

It was the same thing I thought, namely that it simply wasn't fair, pretending to be a nasty kidnapper and then coming out and revealing oneself as a mere reporter.

"So we're still no closer to discovering who's behind these kidnappings?"

"Not an inch closer," I agreed.

"Too bad," he said with a sigh.

For a moment we were both silent. On the water, Odelia was going under, having fallen off her skis for the third time. Surprisingly, Joanna was actually the only one who'd managed to stay upright so far. Must be all those books she balanced as an accountant. Clearly worked wonders for her sense of equilibrium.

"Maybe Harriet and Brutus will have better luck," said Dooley.

"I doubt it," I said. "I don't buy Gran's theory about the seductresses being behind this whole thing. No, the real culprit will be on this island, and so far I haven't a clue who it could be."

"It could be Clint Bunda himself."

"But why? Why would Clint abduct his own contestants?"

"Maybe he collects them?"

"Collects them?"

"Well, some people collect stamps or baseball cards or comic books. Maybe Clint is the kind of man who collects reality show contestants?"

It was a thought, of course. Though it's a lot harder to collect women than it is to collect stamps or baseball cards or comic books. Not to mention illegal. Then again, it takes all kinds of people to make the world go round, so maybe Dooley was onto something.

"Let's take a closer look at his room," I suggested therefore. Frankly there's only so long you can watch people falling into the water and having to be rescued by the Chippendales.

So Dooley and I made our way to the staff villa, and entered unnoticed. The villa was pretty much emptied out, most of the technical crew at the waterfront, making sure the candidates' escapades were captured in technicolor and perfect surround sound.

Once upstairs, we found that Clint had closed his door. We quickly found a workaround, though: we snuck into a neighboring room, and proceeded onto the balcony. Just like the first floor it was of the wraparound variety, and we easily moved from room to room, this time having more luck, as people tend to leave their windows open in these hot climes.

And it was as we arrived on the fourth balcony that we hit pay dirt. Actually we hit upon the producer himself, taking a nap on his balcony, his hat draped over his eyes.

So we snuck into his room and started our silent inspection. Unfortunately I didn't find anything to raise a red flag that this man was our man: no strange communications or discarded messages indicating Clint had a secret and highly illicit hobby.

I even hopped onto his desk to inspect his laptop, but ended up scrolling through an endless list of emails, finding nothing particularly incriminating except a penchant for off-color jokes.

And just when I'd opened his Facebook, a knock sounded at the door, and Dooley and I quickly scooted under the bed.

"Mr. Bunda!" a voice called out. "Mr. Bunda, sir!"

"Grmbl," was the response from the balcony. Moments later the big guy came stumbling in, still sleepy, and opened the door. "Oh, it's you," we heard him say, and I snuck a look from underneath the bed. It was a skinny, pale-looking guy with pockmarked face I thought I'd seen before. One of the technicians.

"There's a problem with one of the feeds," said the guy.

"Feeds?" grumbled Clint with the air of a man who's just been roused from a relaxing slumber. I knew just how he felt, having been in the same position many a time myself.

"The feed from Jackie Copley's bedroom," said the techie. "It cuts in and out."

"Well, then fix it," said Clint irritably. "They're all out on the water right now, so you better fix it before they get back."

"It's just that…"

"Just what?"

"What if Miss Copley walks in just as I'm fixing the cameras?"

"Ask Frank to go with you. Tell him to wait outside and watch out for Jackie. Tell him to whistle if she walks up."

"Whistle, sir?"

"You do know how to whistle, don't you, Rick? You just put your lips together and blow." And to show what he meant, he proceeded to give us a demonstration. A copious amount of spittle proceeded from his lips, hitting his technician, but no sound came.

"I don't think he knows how to whistle, Max," said Dooley.

"No, I don't think so either," I said, thoroughly amused by the scene.

"Maybe I'll tell Frank to make the sound of a bird, sir," said Rick, who wasn't convinced by this botched demonstration.

"Do whatever you like," grumbled Clint.

"Do you know an indigenous bird, sir?"

"What kind of bird now?"

"Indigenous to these parts, sir? We don't want to draw suspicion by making the sound of a bird that doesn't inhabit these islands, sir."

"Oh, go to blazes!" Clint barked, and slammed the door in the techie's face, thus ending the conversation with the kind of finality the producer of a hit show likes to see.

It also ended Dooley and my excursion into the life of Clint Bunda, as I didn't think the man was the kind of collector Dooley had taken him for. The only things the man seemed to collect were insults and naps, as he went straight back to his balcony, and moments later the telltale sound of loud snores told us the coast was clear, so we skedaddled, not exactly with our tails between our legs, but very nearly so.

When were we finally going to catch a break?

26

When we arrived downstairs, we passed a room whose door was ajar. Inside, Rick was explaining to a guy I assumed was Frank of how they were going to go about restoring the camera feed from Jackie's bedroom.

"So you hide in the bushes and the moment Jackie arrives you make this sound," he said, then tapped a key on a computer and the sound of birdsong filled the air.

It was a strange, whoop-whoop-whooping kind of sound, like a cuckoo but different.

"It's the mating call of the hoopoe," Rick explained. "That way Jackie won't suspect a thing. Now give it a try."

Frank, a heavyset guy with no hair on top of his head and the fringes tied back in a ponytail, pursed his lips and tried to mimic the sound of the hoopoe. It wasn't even close. In fact it sounded more like a kettle going on the boil.

"No, Frank. You're not even trying," said Rick.

"Why can't I just whistle?" asked Frank plaintively.

"You can whistle?" asked Rick, sounding surprised.

"Sure. Who can't?" And he produced a healthy whistle,

this time without covering his colleague in a waterfall of spittle.

"Okay, I can live with that," said Rick.

"Or I could do the Imperial March," said Frank as he and Rick walked out. And without waiting for a response he started singing some bombastic-sounding snatch of music.

"No, no, no!" said Rick. "That's not how it goes. John Williams specifically added those grace notes. Here, let me show you."

And while the two geeks walked off, to make sure Jackie's nocturnal escapades were picked up for the audience's edification, if not titillation, Dooley and I snuck into the room and found ourselves gazing at a wall of screens, feeds visible from all over the resort. They were all neatly labeled, too: Odelia's bedroom, Odelia's bathroom, Odelia's living room...

"Oh, my God," I said. "This is a voyeur's paradise. If Norman Bates saw this, he'd break into song and dance."

"They're filming everything," said Dooley, awed by this flagrant intrusion of privacy. "They even film her when she's in the bathroom."

"I think there's probably laws against that," I said as I checked the other screens. All four candidates were there, but also the four male contestants, and all of the seducers and seductresses. And on top of that many public areas, too, like the plazas, the bars, the toilets behind both plazas, the beaches...

"This must be the main control room," I said. "Where all the feeds come in."

"There must be hours and hours of footage," said Dooley.

"Must be a nightmare to edit."

A scene attracted my attention. It was Odelia sitting on the beach with seducer Mike. And they appeared to be very cozy indeed.

Dooley must have seen it, too, for he said, "I don't like

that, Max. Odelia and this Mike guy? Soon she'll dump Chase and Mike will move in with us. And what if he doesn't even like cats?" A note of panic had entered his voice as he talked. "Maybe he'll demand she get rid of us, and then where does that leave us? Out on the street. Or at the pound!"

"Let's not get ahead of ourselves," I said soothingly. "Odelia is simply chatting with Mike, probably trying to find out what he knows about the missing women."

"Look, Max!" Dooley cried, and pointed to another screen. It depicted Chase, also seated on the beach, over on the other island, chatting with a blonde of impressive measurements. "It's happening, Max! Passion Island is breaking up our couple!"

"Not a chance," I said, though I had to admit both Odelia and Chase looked very cozy chatting with people that weren't their significant other. "I'm sure they're just talking. And there's nothing against talking, is there?"

On yet another screen, I saw Gran and Scarlett seated at the bar, chatting. I wondered what they were talking about. Possibly Gran's theory about the seductresses being behind this whole kidnapping scheme.

🐾

"We've got to do something, Scarlett. I'm telling you, this whole thing is going to hell in a handbasket if we don't interfere now!"

"Relax, Vesta," said Scarlett as she sipped from her drink. "Mh. This stuff is pretty good. What's in this, darling?" she asked the bartender, a handsome young man she'd taken a shine to.

"Banana rum, pineapple juice, Blue Curaçao and cream of coconut, ma'am," said the kid.

Scarlett giggled and said, "Ma'am. Do I look like a ma'am

to you?" She placed a hand on the man's arm and squeezed his bicep appreciatively. "Call me Scarlett."

"Um, all right…" said the kid, his eyes taking in Scarlett's impressive bust.

"Scarlett!" said Vesta. "Stop trying to seduce that kid and listen to me. If we don't get Chase out of the claws of that Donna person we're going to lose him, you hear me?"

"Not a chance. That boy loves your granddaughter. He's not going to risk it all just for the chance to dive into bed with that floozie."

"That floozie's got her sights set on him, and she's working him for all she's got. Men are weak, Scarlett. You know it and I know it. Remember Jack?"

"Oh, do I remember Jack!" said Scarlett with a grin. Then, as she saw Vesta's thunderous expression, she dropped the smile. "Look, Chase is not like other men. He's one of the good guys. He's not going to cheat on your granddaughter. No way."

"He doesn't want to cheat, but he won't be able to help himself. But I have a plan."

Scarlett rolled her eyes. "Here we go again."

"Listen to me!"

"I'm listening, I'm listening!"

"We have got to make sure he doesn't sleep with the woman, so here's what we're going to do." And as she explained her plan in great detail, earning herself another eyeroll in the process, she couldn't help but hope that on the other island someone was offering the same courtesy to Odelia, cause if she succumbed to the charms of this Mike guy Chase had mentioned, all was well and truly lost.

*I*n spite of the fact that she'd sucked in more seawater than strictly necessary, and had spent more time in the water than on her skis, Odelia discovered to her surprise that she'd had a good time. She wasn't naturally inclined to try out new things, especially when they could potentially end in terminal consequences to life and limb, but the water skiing was a lot more fun than she'd anticipated.

Looking and feeling like a water chicken, she returned to her villa to wash the brine from her hair and skin, and get dressed for dinner. Francine had announced she had a surprise for them, and she had a feeling she knew exactly what this surprise entailed.

Date night.

And since the seducers were the ones taking the initiative she saw a late-night date with seducer Mike in her immediate future.

She reckoned she could have hit it worse. Mike was a nice guy. They'd chatted a little on the beach, after she'd finally decided she'd had enough of the water skiing experiment. He worked as a male model for a New York agency and had joined Passion Island to raise his profile with the company and land more lucrative gigs. He wasn't necessarily a lady killer, though, and had admitted he actually had a girl back home, and she'd never forgive him if he hooked up with a contestant.

So she was pretty much safe with him, knowing he wouldn't hit on her. Or at least not too hard.

As she walked up the path to her villa, she was waylaid by Jack Davenport, who'd clearly been lying in wait.

"Can I talk to you?" he asked, looking left and right as if expecting company.

"Sure. What's on your mind?"

"Not here," he said, and took her by the elbow, leading her behind the villa. "I disabled the feed before I came out here," he explained.

Odelia had slung a towel around herself, but was eager to get inside and take that shower, so she said, "Better make it quick. I need to get ready for dinner."

"Listen," he said, lowering his voice. "It's about Joanna."

"Joanna? What about her?"

"You know how I spied on all of the candidates, right? Back in Bangkok? Making sure they were couples or not? So when I was checking up on Joanna and her boyfriend she slipped out of bed in the middle of the night to make a mysterious phone call in the bathroom. It was really annoying, cause I wanted to leave their hotel room and I couldn't. I was hiding behind the curtains the whole time, and getting a crick in the neck."

"What mysterious phone call?"

"I don't know, but it was obvious she didn't want her boyfriend to overhear her. I didn't think anything of it at the time, but with what you told me about women going missing…" He arched a meaningful eyebrow.

"You think she's involved somehow?"

"It's worth looking into, don't you think?"

Odelia nodded slowly. "Thanks. I'll try to bring it up with her." She wondered how, though. She couldn't very well confess that she'd made a pact with the intrusive tabloid reporter.

"Oh, and one other thing," said Jack as Odelia started for the front of the villa. "Better watch your back. I looked into the profiles of the five women who disappeared and they all have one thing in common."

"What?"

"They're the spitting image of… you."

"Yeah, I know."

As Odelia luxuriated under the spray of the rainfall shower head, she mused on Jack's words. He was right. Of all four candidates she was the only one who resembled the type the five missing women represented. Which meant that whoever this kidnapper was, he might come after her next. And in spite of the heat of the shower, she suddenly shivered, and wished Chase wasn't on a different island, separated by a large swath of sea.

Now that she came to think of it, all of her allies were far away: Chase and Gran were one island over, Uncle Alec was in Hampton Cove, and her parents were in Europe.

Then, as she toweled then tied the towel on top of her head, she smiled when Max and Dooley came ambling into the bedroom.

At least she had two cats in her corner.

"So what did you guys get up to today?" she asked.

"Oh, this and that," said Max airily.

"We saw you on the beach with Mike," said Dooley, not so

airily. "Are you and Mike getting married, Odelia? Is he moving into our house soon and is Chase moving out?"

Two pairs of cat eyes stared at her accusingly, and she laughed. "Oh, you guys. Of course not. Mike is just a friend. Well, not even a friend. More of an acquaintance." She made a conscious effort not to move her lips too much, in case the cameras picked up on it. "Shall I let you in on a little secret?"

Both cats nodded eagerly.

"Mike is engaged to be married. He only took this job to improve his chances to land better jobs back home so he can get married to his high school sweetheart. So there's nothing for you to worry about."

They both heaved sighs of relief, especially Dooley, who was something of a worrywart sometimes. "I really thought he was moving in!" Dooley cried, now also smiling. "And I figured that if he doesn't like cats he'd kick us both out and we'd have to spend the rest of our days at the pound!"

"No pound for you, my sweet," said Odelia, and finished dressing. She told the cats about her meeting with Jack, and they offered to spy on Joanna to see what she was up to. She decided not to mention she fit the profile of the abducted women to a tee. No need to get them all worked up about it.

"You should have seen the setup these people have," Max said as he stretched out on the bed. "An entire bank of screens, wall to wall, showing footage from dozens and dozens of cameras planted all over the two resorts."

"Yeah, they can see everything you do," Dooley chimed in. "It's a little creepy."

"It's very creepy," Odelia said.

"Jackie's camera broke," Max continued. "And two technicians named Rick and Frank had to go and fix it before tonight. It seemed like a big deal to Clint."

"I think they're expecting fireworks tonight," Odelia said as she checked herself in the mirror. She'd opted for a simple floral dress that made her look less like a femme fatale and more like the girl next door. She figured she was done playing the perfect candidate and was going to be more herself from now on.

"We're having fireworks tonight?" asked Dooley, surprised. "I don't like fireworks. It makes me want to pee."

"I don't mean actual fireworks," she said, wondering what to do with her hair. "I mean..." She directed a glance down at Dooley, who was eyeing her intently. "Um..."

"What Odelia means to say is that Jackie and the boy she likes are probably going to spend some time together," said Max, treading carefully. "Because they like each other so much."

"But doesn't Jackie like her own boyfriend anymore?"

"Well, her own boyfriend has been very naughty over on the other island and he's been, um... kissing another girl. So now Jackie is upset and she's decided to, um..."

"Kiss another boy," said Dooley, nodding. "To get even."

Odelia gave Dooley a look of surprise. "Correct," she said.

"I watch a lot of soaps with Gran," Dooley explained. "Women on General Hospital do that kind of thing a lot. But sooner or later they forgive their boyfriends and then they get married. So I'm sure that's what'll happen with Jackie and Gary. When the show is over they'll kiss and make up and live happily ever after."

Somehow Odelia doubted whether Dooley's rosy world view would come true for Jackie, but she nodded. "I'll bet you're right, Dooley."

"Of course I'm right. Though there's also a small chance Jackie will end up getting pregnant and discover that Gary isn't the father but Gary's long-lost twin brother is, and she'll end up drinking a lot of alcohol and crashing her car and needing plastic surgery and falling in love with the trauma surgeon over at the hospital who'll turn out to be her father." He shrugged. "Happens all the time."

Odelia frowned and reminded herself to tell Gran not to watch her soaps in front of Dooley again. It clearly was having an adverse effect on the poor cat.

28

*T*hat evening, dinner wasn't the usual laid-back affair. Instead, different nooks had been arranged, where different seducers sat down with the four contestants for their first date night. Which seducer got to date which contestant had been left to the show's producers to decide, and in Odelia's case Mike was the lucky boy. Or unlucky, depending on how you looked at it.

Dooley and I had taken up position nearby, making sure nothing untoward was happening. You could call us our human's keepers. Odelia may have told us she wasn't interested in dating this male model, but that didn't stop us both from worrying.

For once I heartily agreed with Dooley that he had reason for concern. I liked Chase, and didn't enjoy the prospect of Odelia performing a switcheroo and replacing him with this Mike character.

"He doesn't look like a cat hater," said Dooley as we closely observed the man.

"Appearances can be deceiving, Dooley," I reminded him. "He could be on his good behavior now, but the moment he moves in with Odelia he could turn out to be some kind of Cruella De Ville, only in his case out to skin cats not Dalmatian puppies."

"You're right," said my friend. "We have to watch him like a hawk. Did you know that hawks can spot a prey from a hundred feet? Amazing creatures, hawks. They eat mice."

Dooley watches a lot of Discovery Channel, which is preferable to watching Gran's batch of daily soap operas. It sometimes leads to strange interludes in our conversations, though.

"Speaking of mice," I said, "did you ever find out why Hector prefers our basement over Marge's?" I couldn't help but think back to those halcyon days when we were still blissfully unaware of Passion Island and missing women, the days before Kimmy had entered our lives and dragged us out to Koh Samui Island with its palm trees and scorching heat.

"Odelia says it's because they know we won't harm them," said Dooley.

"Brutus and Harriet wouldn't harm them either," I said, frowning. I didn't like these disparaging notions about my mouse-hunting prowess being bandied about so loosely.

"No, but Harriet at least tried to catch them once, remember?"

"That wasn't Hector and Helga. That was a different family of mice."

"Odelia thinks mice talk. And word must have spread about Harriet being the kind of cat who doesn't waste time hunting any rodent intruder."

"Mh," I said dubiously.

"It's a good thing, Max," said Dooley. "If the mice of Hampton Cove all think you're a softie, it says a lot about you. You should take it as a compliment."

"I'm not sure that a reputation of being soft on mice is necessarily a good thing, Dooley. What if all the mice of

Hampton Cove decide to come and live with us? Where would that leave us? Out on the street, probably."

He threw me a worried glance, in between his stares at Mike. "In that case I hope the house won't be overrun with mice by the time we get back."

"Uncle Alec said he'd drop by once a week to water the plants," I reminded him.

We both shared a look of concern now. Uncle Alec isn't exactly the most conscientious homeowner. His own place is usually a mess of epic proportions, so his promise to watch Odelia and Marge's houses was probably not such a good thing.

"Look, we made a pact," I reiterated a point I'd had to explain to a lot of cats since its inception. "And Hector is not the kind of mouse who'd renege on a promise once given."

Though truth be told his kids didn't always seem to adhere to the pact, judging from the food that kept disappearing from Odelia's fridge and pantry at regular intervals.

"Max!" suddenly Dooley cried. "He's going in! He's going to try and kiss her!"

Dooley was right. Right before our very eyes Mike was leaning across the table, which was set for a romantic dinner for two, complete with candles and the resort's very best china, a string quartet's gentle tones oozing from the speakers.

"As we practiced, Dooley," I said crisply. "On your mark—ready, set, GO!"

And as one cat we jumped on top of the offending lover boy.

❧

*O*delia had to admit that Mike made for good company. Frankly she was feeling a little drowsy. She still hadn't fully recovered from the jet lag, and spending the afternoon on the water practicing a sport at which she was an absolute novice had made her particularly sleepy. But Mike was easy to talk to, and funny to boot. And when she told him she was going to turn in early he didn't mind one bit.

"It might earn me a pretty harsh rebuke from Francine but I don't care," he said as he held his glass of wine and clinked it against hers.

"Rebuke? Why?"

"The whole idea of this dinner is that it ends in a win for Team Seducers," he said with a grin. "And it would earn me a pretty hefty bonus."

"This show is really immoral on so many levels," said Odelia, a little disgusted. "They're actually paying you money if you manage to get into bed with me?"

"There's a bonus system," he explained. "First base nets us a cool hundred, second base two hundred, and so on and so forth. It's pretty elaborate."

"How much for nookie?" she asked.

"A thousand. Two for a repeat performance and another two for every night after that. So you see, it adds up."

"That's pretty sick," she said, shaking her head. "Like legalized prostitution."

"Yeah, if I'd known about it I probably wouldn't have signed up. Problem is, they don't tell you from the beginning. They only let you in on the bonus system once you're already here and fully committed. It's tough to walk out if you've gone to all the trouble of putting your life on hold for the duration of the show."

"Well, I'm very sorry, Mike," said Odelia. "But you're not

going to win anything by going after me. Not one cent, I'm afraid."

"And like I said, that's perfectly fine with me. I'm not here to cash in. Besides, I don't want to lose the respect of my girl. She'll be watching this and so will her family, and mine. Do you want a refill?" He leaned over to grab the bottle, and all of a sudden, out of nowhere, two furry fiends came flying, and attached themselves to Mike. One furry fiend jumped on top of his head, while the other hit his chest like a cannonball.

Uttering a loud scream, Mike toppled over and fell to the floor.

"Max! Dooley!" Odelia cried, springing to her feet. "Get off him!"

"But he's trying to kiss you!" Max yelled, seated on the unfortunate seducer's chest.

"He wasn't. Now get off!"

They did as they were told, and Odelia helped Mike to his feet. He looked more startled than hurt, though his nose was bleeding where apparently Dooley had bitten him.

"What was that?!" he yelped.

"My cats. They must have thought you were trying to, um… Well, they're very protective."

"They're crazy!" he squealed, checking his chest for puncture marks. "Crazy cats!"

And with these words, he walked off, a little unsteadily.

"I'm sorry!" she yelled after him, but he was mumbling to himself under his breath.

"We thought he was moving in for a kiss," Max explained.

She sat down and arched an eyebrow in her cat's direction. "I guess I should praise myself lucky that you never took a dislike to Chase. You might have killed him."

"We would never attack Chase," said Dooley earnestly. "We like Chase. Chase is great."

In spite of the ruinous ending to her evening, she smiled. "Your intentions were good, but next time please don't attack my dates."

"There will be others?" asked Max, startled.

"After this? Probably not."

Members of the production team came running now. They must have seen everything on their monitors. In the distance she could see Mike receiving first aid, and Kimmy was by her side, fussing over her and asking if she was all right.

"Did you get all of that on tape?" asked Odelia.

Kimmy grinned. "Oh, yeah. I have a feeling your cats are going to be pretty famous after this."

"You hear that, guys?" asked Odelia. "You're going to be famous. They'll turn you into memes."

Dooley's eyes went wide. "But I don't want to be turned into memes! I want to live!"

2 9

*O*ver on Koh Phangan, the men's island, things weren't progressing quite as Harriet had anticipated. She'd hoped to get a lot of screen time, and had positioned herself in the picture as much as felinely possible.

While the men were frolicking in the pool with the seductresses, she'd stuck close to the cameramen, but they'd roundly ignored her attempts to strut her stuff. One had even had the gall to kick in her direction and utter the one cry cats hate more than anything: 'Shoo!'

Wounded to the core of her immortal soul, she'd retreated to her lodgings, which were also Chase's lodgings, and Brutus's, the latter telling her not to take these things personally, as cameramen will be cameramen and apparently this one was as anti-cat as they came.

During the campfire, she'd positioned herself on Chase's lap, and had remained there throughout, until Chase had become all agog at the sight of Odelia sitting on the beach in her bikini chatting with a hunk in trunks and Harriet had been flung from his lap when he'd started gesticulating wildly.

And during Chase's dinner date with Donna, she'd managed to walk into the picture a couple of times, until one of the producers had bodily grabbed her and deposited her elsewhere.

"The gall of these people!" she cried. "To manhandle me. Me!"

"Yeah, that wasn't nice," Brutus agreed.

They were back in Chase's room, where they'd returned after this most recent and infuriating incident.

"I'm going to tell Chase to write a strongly worded email to the producer that this kind of thing can't go on. This island is full of cat haters and something must be done."

"At least they can't cut you from the frame, sweet puss. Or else they'll have to cut Chase, too, and they're not going to do that."

"They can edit me out. These people can do anything. Edit me in or out as they see fit. Just like Stalin."

"Stalin?"

"He used to edit people out of his pictures all the time. At least that's what Dooley told me." She frowned darkly. "If this keeps up I'm going to be deleted from history completely. As if I was never even here!"

"I'm sure it won't come to that," said Brutus soothingly.

"I wouldn't be too sure. These people are capable of anything, even feline deletion!"

Just then, Gran and Scarlett both came bursting into the room.

"Harriet, Brutus!" whispered Gran, as if afraid she might be overheard. "How did Chase's date go?"

"Yeah, how did it go?" Scarlett echoed.

"They kicked me out," said Harriet. "Can you believe it? There I was, strutting my stuff for all I'm worth, and some minion came and grabbed me and told me in no uncertain terms to get lost."

"Huh," said Gran, not really showing the kind of compassion a cat scorned likes to see in her human. "So was there any kissing going on? Things heating up between Donna and Chase?"

"No kissing," said Brutus categorically. "I checked."

"Good," said Gran, satisfied. She turned to her friend. "No kissing," she explained.

"Doesn't mean anything," was Scarlett's prompt response. "They could be kissing up a storm right now, and heading this way for some after-dinner nookie."

"Over my dead body," Gran growled. "Harriet, Brutus. New mission. The moment Donna sets foot in this villa you have my permission to do whatever it takes to get her out again."

Harriet perked up at this. In every cat lurks a touch of the wild. They may have allowed themselves to be domesticated but, unlike the canine species, have managed to retain the hunter's instinct their ancestors possessed. Under normal circumstances a cat tamps down on its primeval instincts, but to give it permission to unleash these urges is like giving a pyromaniac a set of matches and telling him to go and build a nice bonfire.

"Anything at all?" asked Harriet, sheathing and unsheathing her sharp claws.

"Whatever it takes," Gran repeated. "That campfire was a disaster, and it wouldn't surprise me if Chase decided to get some of his own back after watching Odelia schmooze with that musclehead."

"I thought he was very handsome," said Scarlett. "In fact I wouldn't mind making his acquaintance one of these days."

Scarlett had lamented on more than one occasion that the four candidates weren't much to write home about, and she'd much rather have a go at the seducers over on the other island instead. But since beggars can't be choosers she'd decided to help Gran.

"You and I are going to hide under the bed," said Gran now.

"Wait, what?!" cried Scarlett.

"That way we can make sure Chase doesn't do anything stupid. Like cheat on Odelia."

"I'm not crawling under that bed," said Scarlett.

"Fine. You can hide in the closet then."

"How about I hide in the bathroom? When they catch me I can always tell them I got confused. These villas all look the same anyway."

"It's either the closet or the bed. You choose."

"Oh, all right. I'll take the closet. But I'm not staying in there all night. I need my beauty sleep."

"It won't take long, believe me," said Gran with a resolute look on her face.

"So if Chase and Donna walk in, we pounce?" asked Harriet eagerly. "Go for the jugular?"

"Take it easy, princess," said Gran. "We want to scare the woman, not create a bloodbath. No, when they walk in, you create a big fuss. And when that doesn't work, Scarlett and I will come out of hiding and try to talk some sense into the guy."

"It will be hard," said Scarlett. "By the time Chase walks in with Donna he'll be so hot and bothered he could get belligerent when he doesn't get what he wants."

"That's where Brutus comes in." Gran crouched down, causing her knees and hips to creak dangerously. "Brutus, you hit Chase with anxious puss face. You know, like Puss in Boots from those Shrek movies."

Brutus frowned.

"No, not like that."

"I don't think I've seen that movie," he said, looking a little confused.

"Brutus doesn't really do anxious," said Harriet. "He does scary very well, though."

"Fine, you do scary and Harriet, you do anxious puss."

"I don't do anxious either," said Harriet haughtily. "It isn't in my repertoire, I'm afraid."

"Oh, fine! So you both do scary." Gran then slid underneath the bed. "The things I do for my granddaughter," she muttered.

Scarlett disappeared into the bathroom and Vesta yelled after her. "Where are you going?"

"Touch up my makeup. I want to look good for the cameras."

"Get back here."

"Yes, boss," said Scarlett, tripping back into the room.

"Now into the closet with you, and be quick about it!" Vesta barked.

Scarlett giggled. "This is so exciting!"

And thus the scene was set.

Now all it took was for Chase to walk in with Donna and the show was a go.

30

I was feeling slightly embarrassed about the predicament we'd landed our human in. Mike apparently had been spooked to such an extent he wanted to go home, and even Clint had come down to declare the plaza and its surroundings off-limits for cats from now on. And since Dooley and I were the only cats on the island that clearly meant us.

Odelia herself wasn't mad. I think she was even proud of the protective instincts that had guided our misguided attempt to make her remain faithful to her chosen one.

She was also very tired, though, so she'd turned in for the night the moment Mike had been patched up sufficiently and the date had officially been written off as a total loss.

So it was with mixed emotions that I walked into Odelia's villa, Odelia pretty much dead on her feet and Dooley still speculating whether Mike had worn a toupee or not.

"I felt his hair shift when I landed on top of his head," he repeated. "I'm sure he's wearing a hairpiece, Max."

"It could be a weave," I countered. "A hairpiece would

have come off when he was on that speedboat dragging Odelia behind him on her water skis."

"Not when he's glued it in place."

"You don't glue a hairpiece in place, Dooley," I said. "You loosely attach it to your scalp and hope the wind won't pick it up and deposit it on your date's plate."

All this talk of weaves and hairpieces didn't appear to capture Odelia's attention, for she headed straight for the bathroom, fully intent on getting ready for bed.

"I still think it was a toupee," said Dooley.

"Must have been a weave," I argued.

The thought then occurred to me that there was only one way to settle the argument once and for all: we could simply go over to Mike's villa and see for ourselves. It's a rare man who sleeps with a toupee, as it tends to shift when he turns in his sleep. A weave, on the other hand, stays firmly stuck in place.

And as we walked back out of the villa, I briefly wondered if we weren't forsaking our sacred duty as Odelia's watch-cats. Then I figured that with all the cameras watching her every move, it would be a very dumb kidnapper indeed to try and snatch her now.

Five minutes later Dooley and I were gazing in through the window to see if Mike the seducer was a toupee man or a weave man.

As luck would have it, he came walking out of the bathroom just when we arrived. And much to my surprise, he was rocking a Jason Statham, cleanly shaven dome and all.

"See!" said Dooley triumphantly. "It was a toupee!"

"Touché," I murmured, gracious in defeat.

And just as we were about to hop down from the windowsill, much to my surprise a second person came walking out of the bathroom. It was Jackie, and she was only wearing a towel, and as she dropped it, she was wearing even less.

I gulped, and so did Dooley.

"Oh, my," I said. "Looks like our friend Mike has gotten over his cat-induced trauma pretty quick."

And as Jackie joined Mike in bed, I gulped some more, and then, for some reason, my right hind leg suddenly developed a cramp and shot out, neatly hitting Dooley in the buttocks and sending him flying off the windowsill. These kinds of R-rated scenes were not fit for the likes of him.

"What happened?" he asked, having neatly landed on his feet.

"I don't know," I said, joining him on the deck. "I got a sudden cramp in my leg."

The sound of the gong echoed through the air, but judging from the giggling sounds inside the room, Mike nor Jackie seemed to mind.

"We better get back to Odelia," I said, before Dooley could hop onto that windowsill to watch the sequel.

Dooley immediately picked up on my hint. "You think she's all right?"

"Let's go and find out," I said, and soon we were trotting back to our own villa.

We hadn't even set foot inside when a loud scream rocked me to the core, and we covered the last couple of yards in a flash.

Inside the bedroom, Odelia sat up, looking dazed. Next to her, I recognized one of the other seducers. I think his name was Fred.

Fred was grinning, even as Odelia was looking at him as if she'd just discovered dog poo on her shoe.

"What the hell do you think you're doing?!" she cried.

The anatomically gifted young man grinned even wider,

then shrugged. "I just figured, with Mike out of the way... Nothing ventured, nothing gained, right?"

"Wrong," said Odelia decidedly, and slapped the guy across the face so hard the sound echoed through the room and made even me wince at the impact.

"Hey! What did you have to go and do that for!" Fred yelled.

"Out!" said Odelia. "Get out!"

"Hold your horses," said the guy, but did as he was told. "If you didn't want to hook up why did you sign up for the show?" he grumbled.

"Out!" she repeated, her voice ringing in my ears.

"I'm going, I'm going," he said, and headed for the door. Before walking out, though, he turned and said, "This could have been a night you'd never forget, babe. Your loss."

Odelia picked up the first object that was available and threw it across the room. Unfortunately for Fred it was the iron she'd used to iron her dress earlier in the evening. It hit the guy in the face with a clunking sound and he went down hard.

"Oops," said Dooley, when the avid seducer didn't come up.

"Looks like this will be a night *he'll* never forget," I said.

Just then, a loud gong sounded, reverberating through the room. It was the second gong of the night, and I had a sneaking suspicion it was triggered by the presence of Fred in Odelia's bed. Even though nothing had happened—apart from him getting knocked out cold—according to the rules it was still a breach.

Looked like Odelia wasn't going home with an extra 50.000 in her bank account.

145

31

Vesta wasn't exactly feeling on top of the world. In fact she was feeling at the bottom of the world, or at least the bed. Dust bunnies tickled her nostrils, and she wondered briefly if the dark shape she saw near the wall could be a dead cockroach or, worse, a live one.

The closet creaked open, and Scarlet loudly hissed, "He's taking his sweet time, that grandson of yours!"

"He's not my grandson yet!" she hissed back.

And she was starting to wonder if Chase was really worth the aggravation. He was a great guy, sure, but there were lots of great guys in the world. And if Chase and Odelia couldn't be trusted with an island full of seducers and seductresses maybe their bond wasn't to be and she was simply wasting her time trying to protect him from making a mistake.

Suddenly she heard the sound of voices approaching. "Get back in your closet, you!" she loud-whispered, and Scarlett did as she was told and closed the door again, but not before emitting an excited giggle. Clearly she was loving every minute of this.

The door to the villa opened, and she heard the telltale

sound of shuffling feet. They'd arrived. Now all she needed to do was wait until they were both in bed and then she was going to pop out from underneath and give Chase a good talking-to.

"Ooh, Chase, you're so sweet!" a woman cooed, and Vesta pressed her lips together.

"It's Donna!" Scarlett said, opening the closet a crack. "I knew it!"

"Get back in there!" Vesta returned.

"Can I offer you something?" Chase was saying. "Wine, beer… something stronger?"

The son of a gun! Shamelessly liquoring up his conquest!

She had half a mind to crawl from under the bed and leave them to it. He didn't deserve Odelia, that much was obvious.

The sound of voices continued, and as Vesta tried to pick up words, she was also keenly aware of the passage of time, as it seemed to take Chase an awfully long time to make his move. Unless he planned to conclude his business on the living room couch. She didn't think so. Chase had always struck her as an old-fashioned kind of guy, and old-fashioned kind of guys still preferred bedding their conquests in their actual beds.

She must have dozed off, then, for when she woke up, the room was awfully quiet, and she wondered if she'd missed her window of opportunity.

She directed a glance at the closet, but of course she couldn't see if Scarlett was still in there or not.

"Harriet!" she whispered, but Harriet was a no-show. "Brutus!" she tried, but once again there was no response.

Dang it. What was going on? Had she slept through the whole thing?

She decided to find out the only way she knew how: by checking the bed for signs of Donnas.

So she crawled from under the bed with some effort, probably covered in dust bunnies from head to toe, and raised her head to check the bed. There clearly was someone asleep in there, and possibly two.

Her face set, she took executive action and jumped into bed, intent on catching the lovers in the act.

"Gotcha!" she yelled.

"Eek!" Chase screamed.

"Gotcha!" Scarlett cried as she hopped into the bed from the other side.

"Eeeek!" Chase yelped, and turned on the light.

Vesta, blinking against the sudden blaze, searched around for Donna.

"Where are you hiding, you trollop!" she said. "Come out now!"

"Yeah, come out now!" Scarlett echoed, clearly having a ball.

"What are you doing?!" Chase said, looking startled as he wrapped the sheet closer to his chest, staring at the two old ladies having hopped into bed with him out of the blue.

"Where is she?" asked Vesta, wagging a menacing finger in the cop's face.

"Yeah, where is the floozie?" asked Scarlett.

"What floozie? What are you talking about?!"

"Donna. I know you're hiding her somewhere," said Vesta.

"Donna? There is no Donna. I sent her home after her third martini and after pumping her for information on the missing women. She was best friends with one of them so I figured she might know what happened to her friend."

Vesta stared at the guy, a little dumbfounded. "You mean you weren't planning on sleeping with the woman?"

"What?! Of course not! I'm in love with Odelia. Why would I want to sleep with Donna?"

"Oops," said Scarlett, making herself comfortable on her side of the bed.

"Yeah, oops," said Vesta, also settling back against the backboard.

Then, as they sat side by side, two seductresses and one contestant, suddenly a loud gong sounded. It was the third gong of the night, this time announcing that one of the men had been unfaithful.

"I think that was your gong, Chase," said Vesta, a little sheepishly.

"Yeah, sorry about that," said Scarlett.

Chase heaved a deep sigh. "Guess I'm not going home with that big prize after all."

"At least you found out something about the missing women, right?" said Gran.

"No. Donna didn't know anything about that."

"Too bad," muttered Vesta.

"We're famous now," said Scarlett. "Most famous trio in the history of Passion Island."

Chase groaned and buried his head in his hands.

I was starting to get the sense that Passion Island wasn't the kind of place a young and innocent mind like Dooley's should necessarily be subjected to. People were jumping into bed left, right and center, and if they weren't huffing and puffing under the cover of a single sheet they were hotting up the dance floor, or steaming gently in the sauna or coming to a slow boil in the jacuzzi. It's one thing to be my friend's keeper, but another to have to labor under circumstances that are a lot less than ideal.

So I had half a mind to tell Odelia to call the whole thing off and return to the safety and comfort of Hampton Cove, if it weren't for the fact that Odelia is one of those people that hates to leave a job before it's well and truly done.

She hadn't yet gotten to the bottom of this baffling mystery of the disappearing women, and so prematurely leaving the island simply wasn't in the cards.

Once again half the production crew had come running the moment they saw Fred take an iron to the noggin and go down for the count.

"What happened?!" Kimmy asked as she surveyed the scene.

"He tried to seduce me," said Odelia simply.

Kimmy's jaw dropped, then she spoke the immortal words, "Are you planning on taking out the entire field of seducers or do you want to leave a couple for the competition?"

"It was an accident," Odelia explained, looking appropriately mortified.

"An accident is when you slip on a bar of soap," said Kimmy. "This?" She gestured to the fallen seducer, who was being tended to by the team's nurse. "This is overkill."

Odelia winced at the mention of the word kill. "I'm sorry. He wouldn't take no for an answer, and I guess I got a little upset, so I just reached for the first thing I could find."

"Good thing it wasn't a knife or he'd be dead." Kimmy then broke into a wide grin. "I have to say I admire your touch, honey. If every guy who doesn't take no for an answer took an iron to the head the world would be a better place. And a lot safer for women."

"Did you hear that gong earlier?" asked Odelia. "Was that the men's gong?"

Kimmy nodded. "I'm sorry to have to tell you, but I'm afraid the gong sounded for your boyfriend."

"Oh, no!"

Kimmy's smile didn't diminish. Quite the contrary.

"Why are you smiling! Chase just cheated on me!"

"Technically, yes, but I think you'll find that actually he didn't."

"What do you mean?"

"Well, I shouldn't be telling you this, but he was caught in bed with your grandmother and your grandmother's friend, and from what I understand it was all one big misunderstanding. They were trying to catch him in the act with

Donna, and ended up getting caught in the act themselves—
the act of giving him a tongue-lashing, that is."

"You're kidding, right?"

"No, I'm not. I saw it with my own eyes. The techies were
laughing so hard they were practically rolling on the floor."
She rubbed Odelia's back. "I gotta tell you, this is shaping up
to be the most interesting season yet, and it's all thanks to
you and Chase."

"Kimmy, can I ask you something?"

The production assistant turned serious. "Did you
discover a lead?"

"Well, Jack claims that Joanna could be up to something."
And in a few words she explained what Jack had discovered.

"I'll look into it," Kimmy promised. "Keep up the good
work—though try not to knock out all of our seducers. We
still need them."

Odelia sank down onto the living room couch, as we
watched the nurse rub something under Fred's nose. He
woke up with a start.

"Wha-wha-wha…" he said, then caught sight of Odelia
and his eyes widened considerably. "Get away from me!" he
cried, scrabbling to his feet.

"Easy, buddy," said the nurse. "Let me check those pupils."

"She tried to kill me!"

"That's what you get from crawling into a woman's bed
without being invited," said the nurse, who was the stern and
implacable kind. "Look into the little light. That's it."

And as she examined the guy, he kept darting nervous
glances to Odelia, which told me he was A-okay. Apparently
it took more than a blow to the head to give him pause. He
did need stitches, though, which was a pretty gruesome sight
to behold, I must say.

"So your gong was a false alarm, and Chase's gong was a
false alarm," I told my human when all the hubbub had

finally died down and it was just the three of us again. "Which means you still have a shot at winning this thing."

"I'm not interested in winning this thing, Max," said Odelia. "All I want is to figure out who's kidnapping these women. And I'm still nowhere on that." She yawned. "But tomorrow is another day, and maybe Kimmy will have some luck with Joanna so I'm not going to start despairing just yet. No, sir, I am not."

And with these words, she stumbled into the bedroom, tumbled into the bed, and was soon snoring away like a lumberjack—a fine-boned, fair-haired lumberjack, that is.

And since Passion Island was oddly devoid of cats of any persuasion, and I didn't feel like hanging out with the local creatures of the night, Dooley and I hopped onto the bed and turned in for the night as well.

Like Odelia said, tomorrow was another day, and maybe it would bring us closer to the truth.

And if it didn't, there were still four seducers left for Odelia to take a whack at.

$\mathcal{I}$t took our human some little while to get out of bed and ready for action. As I've indicated before, Odelia is never at her best in the early morning, and usually needs a strong dose of caffeine to get her system into gear. Now, after last night's events, and less hours of sleep than is her custom, she looked like a shadow of her usual chipper self.

Still, her phone call with Chase was waiting, and she didn't want to miss it for the world, so on her feet she was, and staggering toward the bathroom for a refreshing shower.

"At least today we won't run into Scarface, aka Jack Davenport," I told Dooley as I attended to my morning toilette, which consists of applying my raspy tongue to every part of my physique I'm able to reach, while Dooley did the same. He usually finishes quicker, as he doesn't have quite as much acreage to cover. Or maybe his tongue is bigger.

"I wonder what Harriet and Brutus have been up to," said Dooley, proving once again that members of a species are mainly interested in what members of the same species are up to. Cats like to know the latest gossip about other cats, and the same goes for humans.

"I believe Harriet isn't interested in solving this mystery as much as securing herself a part in Cat Passion Island," I said. "Though if she really thinks Clint is crazy enough to create a reality show featuring cats, God help poor Brutus."

It just showed you how far my relationship with Brutus had progressed. When first we met, he'd been a grade-A bully, breezing into our lives with all the cockiness of a cop's cat. Now, after having spent a couple of years as Harriet's helpmeet, he was as docile as a newly born lamb, and even a little catpecked. Or a lot.

"I think Brutus would have preferred to be on this island," said Dooley. "So he could hang out with us."

"Too bad cats don't swim," I said. "Otherwise he could have made the passage and joined us."

"And Harriet, too," said Dooley.

"And Harriet," I agreed after a pause. To be honest there are times when I can do without Harriet's company. She's a dear friend but can be a touch overbearing.

Odelia came out of the shower, a towel wrapped around her slender frame and another towel like a turban around her hair, and started going through her closet in search of something suitable to wear.

"No jogging today?" I asked, surprised.

"No, I'm frankly beat," she said. "If anyone catches me I'll tell them I'm going for my morning walk."

It definitely suited me a lot better than the running thing. I really don't see what's so appealing about the concept of jogging. It makes one sweat profusely and turns one's face beet-red. A very unhealthy habit, if you ask me, and even potentially deadly.

Finally having settled on a simple ensemble of jeans

shorts, crop top and ball cap, we were off to find Chase at the end of our journey.

Once again, we passed through peaks and vales, languidly watched over by the island's tallest mountain, named Khao Pom, and finally arrived at our destination without a hitch or a Scarface arresting our progress.

We all moved into the shack, and Odelia took out her phone and waited until the clock struck seven. On the dot, the gizmo started to vibrate happily.

"Hey, babe," Chase's sonorous voice sounded, and Odelia smiled.

"Hey, Chase. I missed you."

"How are things going over there?"

"Pretty okay, though I managed to bean one seducer last night, and another was attacked by my cats. So I guess it's two-nil for Team Odelia."

"You beaned a seducer? Not the one you were gabbing with on the beach?"

"No, he was jumped by Max and Dooley. But how did you know I was talking to Mike on the beach?"

"Campfire," said Chase curtly. "They made a big production of your tête-à-tête. So was it? A big deal, I mean?"

I could tell that Chase was trying to sound casual, but that watching Odelia chat up one of the seducers must have hit him hard.

"We were just talking," said Odelia. "Mike isn't interested in me, Chase. He's engaged to be married and this is just a way for him to further his modeling career."

Chase blew out a sigh of relief. "I'm so glad we have these daily phone calls. I don't know what I'd do. They make it look as if you and this Mike are practically an item."

"It's what they do," said Odelia, nodding. "It's how they make people lose their heads and do foolish things they later regret."

"I hate this show. I think there should probably be a law against this kind of thing."

"So Kimmy tells me you and Gran and Scarlett had a great time last night?"

Chase uttered a groan. "Two seductresses in my bed, and a gong. My night was a big hit."

"I got a gong, too, only my seducer needed stitches after the stunt he pulled." And in a few words she regaled Chase with the story of seducer Fred and his injudicious initiative.

"Wait till I get my hands on that sneaky little—"

"He's learned his lesson," Odelia said with a laugh. "In fact I have a feeling the entire contingent of seducers will run a mile when they see me coming. Word spreads pretty fast around here."

"Good," said Chase decidedly.

The topic of seducers and seductresses exhausted, they turned the conversation to the topic of the missing women. And Odelia had just started telling Chase what Jack Davenport had said about Joanna, when suddenly a loud banging sound interrupted us.

The door to the shack flew open and revealed Clint Bunda, looking appropriately aggrieved, and accompanied by no less than two cameramen, both pointing their cameras at Odelia, who was holding the phone.

"Chase?" she said now. "I'm going to have to call you back." She carefully hit the disconnect button, then sheepishly grinned at the producer. "Hi, Clint. You're up early."

After the producer had confiscated her phone, and escorted her from the shack, he gave her a thorough dressing-down.

"I could have you sent away for this," he growled, hands on his hips and looking like a disappointed parent. The words 'I'm not angry but I'm disappointed' clearly trembled on his lips.

"I'm sorry," said Odelia, looking as contrite as she could manage. "I miss Chase, and these daily phone calls keep me going."

"The whole point of the show is to keep you separated from your boyfriend!"

"I know. I'm sorry," she repeated, hanging her head.

"Look, I'm going to give you a pass," said Clint. "Just this once. And only because you're our most popular contestant."

Odelia looked up at this. "What do you mean?"

"We've been posting snippets of the footage we've shot so far on social media and our YouTube channel, whetting the public's appetite for the upcoming season, and your clips are consistently number one. In fact the clips of your cats clobbering Mike and you knocking out Fred have gone viral. People can't wait to see you in action, Odelia!"

"Um, that's great, I guess," she said, not knowing exactly how to feel about this.

"So I want you to continue—but no more secret phone calls to the boyfriend, okay?"

"I promise, Clint. I'll be good from now on."

Unless Kimmy had another spare phone she didn't have a lot of choice, did she?

"Listen," he said as he placed a hand on her shoulder and started steering her away from the shack. "If you could keep this up, there might be a bonus in it for you."

"Keep what up?" she asked.

"The public loves what you're doing, so if you could do more of it, they'll lap it up."

"You mean knock out more seducers?"

"No, no, no," he said, shaking his head. "Well, yeah, maybe. I don't know. Just do what you do, and I'll make sure you get the best coverage. I'm talking prime placement on the network's website, paid ads, the works. If I'm not mistaken—and I rarely am—you're going to be this season's star, sweetheart. And we're going to milk it for all it's worth."

She gave the producer a watery smile. She hadn't exactly come to Thailand to be a star, and she had a feeling all this attention might even be detrimental to her chances of solving this case. Detectives rarely work well when placed under the limelight. Being in the shadows, unnoticed, working away in the background is more their thing.

"That's great," she said, without much excitement. "Thanks."

"Don't mention it. You scratch my back and I'll scratch yours." And with a pat on the back, he was off, leaving her to consider her new role as Passion Island's rising star.

Max and Dooley had come trotting up, and they looked

as surprised as she was.

"So you're going to be a reality star now?" asked Max. "Like Kim Kardashian?"

"I doubt it," said Odelia as she started the hike back to the resort at a slower pace than the producer, who'd already disappeared out of sight. "I'll get my fifteen minutes of fame and that'll be it. And a good thing, too. I don't think I'd like that kind of scrutiny."

"You could start your own show," Dooley now suggested. "Keeping Up with the Pooles. I'm sure lots of people would be interested."

"No, thanks," said Odelia. "People don't want to see me talking to my cats and sniffing around town for obscure clues and suspects."

"Gran would like it," said Max. "In fact I'm pretty sure she'd love it."

"Oh, I don't doubt it. But I'd hate to live my life under a magnifying glass, a bunch of people with cameras filming every second of it."

"You do know that reality shows are completely scripted, right?" said Max. "You show the public whatever you want to show. None of it is even remotely real."

"Still, I think I'll pass," she said. Just the thought of her family being on national TV gave her the creeps. Though, as Max had said, Gran would probably love it, and so would Harriet. "Look, we're here to solve a case," she reminded her feline friends. "Not to become famous. So let's focus on figuring out what's going on, shall we?" She had a jacuzzi meeting with the three other contestants scheduled after breakfast, and she hoped to pump her fellow candidates for information, especially Joanna.

"Maybe you can drop by the main villa again," she suggested. "Keep your ears to the ground and see if you can't pick up something valuable."

"Will do," said Max promptly.

It was too bad that she wouldn't be able to coordinate her investigation with Chase, but that couldn't be helped. She did wonder how Clint had found out. She'd been so careful. Then again, he might have simply decided to have her followed, in an attempt to get some extra footage of the show's breakout star.

They'd arrived at the resort, and she decided to head straight to breakfast. She wanted to talk to Kimmy before the others arrived, and tell her what had happened.

She found Kimmy chatting to one of the servers. It was the production assistant's task to make sure the candidates were being treated like royalty, and part of that task was to ensure they were properly fed.

She gave Kimmy a sign and the assistant immediately took the hint and came over.

"I just got busted," she said under her breath, and explained how Clint had confiscated her phone.

"That's bad," said Kimmy. "That means they'll probably send you home for breaking the rules."

"No, they won't. Apparently I'm too popular to kick me off the show."

Kimmy's eyebrows shot up. "Huh. That's a first. Clint has never allowed anyone to get away with such a serious breach before."

Odelia stared at the other woman. "He probably never kept a candidate after she incapacitated a seducer either, right?"

Kimmy slowly shook her head as the significance of Odelia's words sunk in. "You think Clint himself could be involved?"

"You tell me. You've worked with the man for, what, six years?"

"He seems hell-bent to keep you in the show."

"And everyone tells me I'm the spitting image of the five women who went missing."

Kimmy flung a hand to her mouth. "Oh, no!"

"Oh, yes," said Odelia, grim-faced. "It would be so easy for Clint to select a certain type of woman for his show."

"And so easy to make them disappear."

"But why? Why would Clint kidnap the contestants of his own show?"

"I have no idea. But I'll tell you what. His wife is also blond and slender, so he's definitely into the type." Her face displayed a horrified expression. "Oh, God. I'm working for a pervert, aren't I? He kidnaps women he likes and does whatever with them."

"We don't know that for sure, Kimmy," said Odelia. "But I do know your boss makes for a very credible suspect." She suddenly got an idea. "Can't you, you know, sneak into his office and check his laptop or something?"

She didn't mention Max had already sifted through the man's emails and hadn't found anything suspicious. But he'd only had a very narrow window of opportunity to work with. A more thorough search could reveal something incriminating.

Kimmy nodded, looking worried as she clasped her clipboard to her chest. "I'll try to sneak a peek when he's taking his after-lunch nap." She shook her head. "I can't believe this. Clint Bunda. A criminal."

"Let's not jump to conclusions," said Odelia, placing a comforting hand on the young woman's arm. "We need proof before we start throwing around accusations. By the way, have you talked to Joanna yet?"

"No, haven't had the chance."

"I'll talk to her."

"How will you bring up the subject?"

"I don't know, but I'll think of something."

35

*C*hase frowned at his phone, as if it had personally insulted him. All he could think was that another seducer must have thrown himself into Odelia's arms to try and break down her defenses and in the process of fending him off she'd dropped her phone.

Odd, he felt. Ominous. And as he set foot for his villa, only a short walk from the beach where he liked to conduct these early morning phone calls that did so much to cheer him up, he was thinking dark thoughts of Mike and Fred and the other seducers.

He glanced in the direction of the other island, and not for the first time wondered if he shouldn't brave the heaving seas and simply make the swim down there.

He was greeted at the breakfast table by Vesta and Scarlett, who looked a lot rosier and healthy than they had any right to, considering their age and lack of sleep.

"And? All is well on the women's island?" asked Gran.

"She hung up on me," he grumbled as he took a seat. "Probably trying to fend off more seducers. Those guys are on her like bees on a pot of honey."

"So what about the gong?" asked Scarlett.

"And that second gong?" Gran added eagerly.

"First gong was for Jackie, the second was a false alarm. Odelia found a guy named Fred in her bed and kicked him out, then beaned him in the head with an iron. Guy needed seven stitches." He smiled at this. For some reason the image of a seducer named Fred needing to be stitched up bucked him up in no small measure.

"Seven stitches?" said Scarlett, then whistled.

"Yeah, the guy wasn't happy when she turned him down."

"Remind me never to get on your granddaughter's bad side," said Scarlett.

"So you see?" said Vesta. "Nothing to worry about. Your fiancée can handle herself, like I always knew she would."

"I feel like we're wasting our time here," said Chase as he directed a listless glance at Gary, Arthur and Nick, who looked like they hadn't slept a wink last night. Probably too busy entertaining their respective seductresses. "The real action is over on the other island, not here. And Odelia is all alone, facing not only a gang of seducers but probably a dangerous criminal, too." He slammed the table with his fist, causing his fellow contestants to look up in surprise. "I should be over there, dammit!" he growled.

"Odelia isn't all alone. She's got Kimmy," said Vesta. "And she's got Max and Dooley."

"What good are two cats against an army of seducers and a kidnapper?!"

"I've known Odelia all her life," said Scarlett now. "And if there's one thing I know it's that she can look after herself. Don't you worry about her. She'll nail that bastard."

"And if you're really that worried, we could always take the boat and pay her a visit," Vesta remarked as she eyed her omelet suspiciously, as if expecting it to come alive.

Chase looked up at this. "Boat? What boat?"

"The same boat that brought us here," said Vesta. "They make the trip every morning. Probably to bring in supplies and stuff. Is it just me or does this omelet smell funny?"

"It's just you," said Scarlett.

"Why didn't you tell me before!" Chase cried.

"I thought you knew," said Vesta, giving him an owlish look. "You're the big detective guy, aren't you? I always figure you know everything."

Chase threw down his napkin. "Show me."

"Not where there are cameras!" Scarlett said indignantly.

"The boat!"

"Oh." the older lady sounded disappointed, then sighed. "Very well. Come along."

&

"Where are they going?" asked Brutus as they watched Chase, Gran and Scarlett leave the breakfast table.

"Probably back to the villa for a conference," said Harriet.

They were both lazily luxuriating on the edge of the dining room, which wasn't a room as much as an area covered with a thatched roof supported by wooden beams.

Even though it was still early, the temperatures were already rising.

"This ocean breeze is so great," said Harriet with a happy sigh. "I could get used to the climate. Rain is very bad for you, Brutus."

"It is?" asked Brutus.

"Oh, sure. Bad for the bones, and joints, and probably a lot of other things, too." She sighed again. "Maybe we could somehow convince Odelia to move to Thailand?"

"I think I'd miss Hampton Cove."

This surprised Harriet, as Brutus hadn't even known Hampton Cove existed a couple of years ago.

"You'd miss Hampton Cove?"

"Yeah, I would," he confessed. "It may be rainy and cold in the winter, but it's home. It's where my friends are, and… my family."

She smiled. "Yeah, I guess you're right. Even though I can kick Shanille's butt sometimes, and strangle Kingman with my bare paws, and I'm not even going to mention Clarice, who frankly scares the living daylights out of me half the time, it's still home." She looked up. "I kinda miss Max and Dooley. I mean, I know they're only one island over, and we see them all the time, but I still kinda miss them being around, you know."

"Yeah, me, too," said her mate.

They were both quiet for a moment, then Brutus said, "I think I heard them say something about a boat. You don't think they're planning on leaving this island and ferrying over to the next one, do you?"

This had Harriet jerk up. "And leave us behind? Stranded? No way!"

"Pretty sure I heard the word boat."

Harriet's happy mood vanished. "Come, Brutus," she said, and got up.

"Where are we going?"

"We're catching that boat. If they think they can just leave us behind like this, they've got another thing coming."

And then they were hot in pursuit of their treacherous humans.

36

*W*alking back to her villa after breakfast to get changed, Odelia almost bumped into a chunky-looking individual with thick-rimmed glasses who made a strange bird-like sound. The moment she came face to face with him, he grimaced as if he were suffering from acute toothache, then scooted off in the direction of the staff villa.

And as she walked in, she caught a man crawling out of her bedroom window, looking flustered. He was carrying a small toolbox in one hand while he tried to negotiate the window with the other.

When she entered the bedroom, he froze, eyes wide, and broke into a stream of apologies.

"I'm so sorry, Miss Poole. I was just in here to fix one of the cameras. The one in the corner of the room. I'm not supposed to be caught by the contestants, or there will be hell to pay, so if you could please, pretty please, not tell Clint, I'd be so grateful. He doesn't like it when the candidates are reminded this villa is chockablock with cameras in every nook and cranny, filming their every move, which is why we try to keep out of sight, but the darn feed dropped away this morning so I thought now would be a good time while you were having your breakfast."

"It's fine," she said, laughing as she held up a hand to stem the flow of words. "I know you have a job to do, so just go ahead and do it."

"Oh, thank you so much, Miss Poole," said the man, who was skinny, and pale with pretty bad skin. "I hadn't finished when my buddy gave me the alarm but I guess you were too quick for him."

"Oh, so that's what that was, huh? I was wondering why he would be making that strange sound."

"It's the sound of the hoopoe. I've been trying to teach him. I figured people wouldn't notice when we used it. It's the hoopoe's mating cry," he added helpfully as he crawled back in and made for the bed. Frowning, Odelia watched as he stepped on top of the bed and started unscrewing what looked like an innocent circular ornament from the ceiling.

"Is that... a camera?" she asked.

"Um, yeah. Offers a great view of the bed."

"Oh, my God," Odelia muttered.

"See, this is why Clint doesn't want us in here when you guys are watching. He figures you might get upset when you realize how many cameras are rigged up in here."

"Well, Clint is right. It is a little upsetting."

"Fixed," said the guy, sounding apologetic. "I'll be out of your hair now, Miss Poole," he added, and crawled down from the bed again. "Have a nice continuation of your day."

And with these words, he was gone.

Odelia heaved a deep sigh, then headed to the bathroom to get changed for her jacuzzi date with the other contestants.

Now this was exactly why she didn't want to become a

reality star. She didn't think she'd enjoy being scrutinized on a daily basis.

Walking out again, this time dressed in a bikini, she walked down the path on her flip-flops and headed for the spa area.

"Wait up!" suddenly spoke a voice behind her. Turning, she perceived it was Joanna, looking flustered.

"Ready for some jacuzzi fun?" asked Odelia.

"Not really," said Joanna. "I woke up with a headache this morning and had half a mind to stay in bed today."

"The jacuzzi will do you good," said Odelia. "It might release some of the tension."

The soft-spoken redhead fell into step next to her. "Is it true that you knocked out a seducer last night?" she asked, her eyes wide and wondering.

Odelia smiled and nodded. "I found him in my bed, if you can believe it."

"Oh, I can. I found a seducer in my bed, too. I didn't try to kill him, though I had a good mind to."

"Who was it?"

"Antonio, the Italian stallion."

"He's very pushy, isn't he?"

"They're all pushy," Joanna lamented.

"I guess it comes with the territory."

"Don't they realize that kind of behavior won't get them anywhere? On the contrary, it's a real turnoff for most women."

"Not for everyone," said Odelia as they passed Jackie's villa.

"No, I guess not."

"Listen, I happened to be talking to one of the techies this morning, and he told me you were caught cheating on Arthur."

Joanna turned to her, looking shocked. "What?"

"Yeah, in Bangkok. He says you slipped out of bed in the middle of the night and went to visit another man in the next room." It was a long shot, but she felt it might do the trick.

"I did not!" Joanna cried, indignant.

"So you didn't crawl out of bed in the middle of the night?" asked Odelia pointedly. "Cause this guy swears up and down they filmed you."

"They were filming us at the hotel?"

"Yeah, I guess they were."

Joanna didn't speak for a moment. She seemed to consider this. "Well, if they had caught me, don't you think they'd have kicked me out of the competition even before it got started?"

"Good point," Odelia agreed.

Joanna swallowed. "I did sneak out of bed that night, but not to visit another man." She eyed Odelia keenly. "Promise you won't tell Arthur?"

"I promise," said Odelia.

"His thirtieth birthday is coming up, which is a big deal, and I'm organizing a surprise party. I've been making arrangements for weeks now. It's supposed to take place when we get back from Thailand. I just wanted to make some final arrangements before they took away my phone. I'm arranging it with Arthur's baby sister, and she can be a bit wishy-washy, so I wanted to have everything nailed down before we left."

"Oh," said Odelia, strangely elated. She'd quietly hoped Joanna was innocent.

"Arthur doesn't suspect a thing. It's going to be a big surprise. I even hired his favorite singer Jimmy Buffett, the Margaritaville guy."

"That sounds great, Joanna," said Odelia. "I think he'll be thrilled."

"Yeah, I hope so. It'll be his last birthday before we tie the knot, and thirty is a big deal, right?"

"Oh, sure," said Odelia. She was relieved Joanna wasn't involved in some kidnapping ring, but also disappointed she'd lost another promising lead. It meant her only suspect now was Clint Bunda, the guy up top.

They'd arrived at the building where the spa was located and walked in. Tina and Jackie were already in the jacuzzi so they joined them. It would have been fun, having a soak with the contestants, if it hadn't been for the three guys filming the whole thing.

How people managed to be spontaneous while being filmed was beyond her. There was probably a trick to it, but so far she hadn't yet mastered it. And neither had the others, as the conversation was wooden and proceeded haltingly along familiar topics like the weather and the quality of the seducers.

And all the while Odelia's mind kept drifting back to Clint.

His words to her that morning suddenly sounded more ominous than before: how she was his new star now. His favorite.

In other words, ripe to be kidnapped!

37

*A*s Odelia had instructed, Dooley and I snuck into the villa where the production team had set up shop, and started snooping around. Frankly I didn't have high hopes that this time would be different than last time we'd inspected this place. Then again, the work of a detective, even a feline one, often consists of small repetitive tasks, not unlike that of a gold digger, who keeps sifting mud until finally one day he hopes to strike gold.

"Do you really think Clint is our guy?" asked Dooley.

Odelia had intimated the producer was her most likely suspect, and for us to look at him with renewed attention.

"I don't know, Dooley, but he is the one who ultimately selects the candidates, so if he's the kidnapper, that would make sense in that he can personally guarantee he'll get what he wants."

"But why would a man kidnap so many women, and all of them so similar? What does he do with them?"

I wasn't prepared to lay it all out for him. It was obvious, though, what a man like Clint would do with all of those women. At least if he was the kind of man Odelia thought he was.

And as we walked into the villa, once again we passed the control room.

"Is it fixed?" asked the man named Frank.

"Yeah, it's fixed all right," said Rick. "No thanks to you, though. You couldn't have given me the signal sooner, could you? She caught me crawling out the window."

"She surprised me! She's a fast walker."

"You were probably playing Pokémon on your phone again," Rick said as he surveyed the wall of screens.

Every single one of the screens was now displaying the jacuzzi, and as I watched in surprise, I saw that most of them were featuring one particular candidate: Odelia. That's what you probably get when suddenly you're deemed the star of the show.

Rick's phone started belting out a tune. I recognized it as the same sound he'd produced before: the mating call of the hoopoe. The guy really had a thing for birds.

We decided to leave them to it. We had other fish to fry, so we repaired upstairs, and once again tried every door until we found one that was unlocked. Soon we were out on the balcony, traipsing past room after room.

"Maybe we should search every room," Dooley suggested.

"Odelia told us to focus on Clint," I reminded him.

"Yeah, but what if Clint is innocent? Odelia has been wrong before."

He was right. Odelia has been wrong more times than she's been right. So I shrugged and we entered the first room we found. If we were going to do this, we might as well go about it in a methodic fashion.

The first room told me that whoever stayed there was not a fan of cleanliness and hygiene, as the place was a big mess.

Clothes were strewn about all over the place, wet towels covered the furniture, candy wrappers littered the floor, and in all of that mess there wasn't a single sign of a laptop, cell phone or tablet computer. Probably the guy or gal who occupied the room liked to keep these possessions close to their person.

We did find a crumpled up note in the wastepaper basket. It appeared to be some kind of sweepstakes: the names of all of the candidates had been written on the left, and on the top of the page a series of names I didn't recognize, except for Rick and Frank. Underneath these names, scores had been awarded each candidate. When tallied, Odelia's name had received the highest score.

"This is a little thick," I said when the significance of the document hit me. "These people are actually holding a wager, presumably putting money on the contestants."

"You mean they're gambling on the show's outcome?" asked Dooley, surveying the document.

"Looks like it," I said. "And Odelia's name is at the top of the list. Meaning they figure she'll probably succumb to the wiles of the seducers more likely than the others."

"Was this before or after she hit Fred in the head?" asked Dooley pointedly.

I smiled. "Probably before. Looks like this person, whoever he is, lost a great deal of money betting on her to fall for Fred's charms."

"Or Mike's charms," Dooley added as he took a tentative sniff at a piece of underwear, then crinkled up his nose when its sheer rankness hit him.

"Let's get out of here," I said. "Plenty of rooms to check and only so much time."

Unfortunately that first room was a harbinger of things to come. It soon became clear that every single member of Clint's team engaged in betting on the candidates' likeliness to fall for this or that seducer or seductress, and the pool must have been a pretty large one, judging from the numbers scribbled on the documents we found in most rooms. It was also the only clue we found, and not the kind of clue we were looking for. And when finally we made our way to Clint's room, the man in charge, we were none the wiser.

We snuck into the big guy's room and were surprised to see it occupied by none other than... Kimmy, eagerly going through the man's personal affairs. She didn't see us come in, as we treaded as softly and surreptitiously as usual, but we saw her clear as day as she dug through Clint's laptop, darting anxious glances at the door from time to time.

"What is she doing?" asked Dooley as we hunkered down behind a chair near the window.

"Spying on her boss," I said.

She probably shouldn't have done that, for at that moment footsteps sounded in the corridor, and suddenly the door swung open and Clint walked in.

Kimmy, an athletic lass, leaped behind the bed, then rolled underneath before Clint caught sight of her. And as she did so, she saw us looking at her, and pressed her index finger to her lips. I nodded once, which appeared to surprise her greatly.

"Now where did I leave the darn thing," Clint muttered as he rooted around his desk. "Ah, there it is," he murmured as he grabbed his laptop. His phone chimed as he opened the door.

"Who is this?" he boomed after a moment's pause. "Her uncle! A cop! Are you kidding me!"

He closed the door again and started pacing the room.

"No, I didn't know Odelia Poole's uncle was a cop. Someone could have told me!" he said, still speaking in that booming voice of his.

The person on the other end must have said something to

upset him, for suddenly he sank down on the bed, making it creak. "She did what?!" he bellowed.

"Uh-oh," I said. "Looks like Odelia's cover is blown."

"We have to do something, Max!" said Dooley. "Clint is going to try and grab her!"

Dooley was right, so we snuck from behind the chair posthaste, then out onto the balcony.

We had to warn Odelia before it was too late!

38

*O*delia had just stepped out of the jacuzzi when there was a sort of commotion nearby. When she glanced over, she saw that Max and Dooley were running full tilt in her direction, but so were Clint and Kimmy. All of them were screaming something she couldn't quite catch.

"What's going on?" asked Tina. "Why are your cats being chased by Clint?"

"Probably stole a fish," Jackie sneered. "Isn't that what cats do? Steal things?"

Obviously Jackie didn't know Max and Dooley very well, Odelia thought. And then she caught what her cats were yelling.

"He knows!" Max cried. "Clint knows about you!"

"Oh, darn," she muttered, and blinked. Clint wouldn't dare grab her with all these witnesses around, would he? There was a reason those women had only been kidnapped after their return from Passion Island. So she decided to bear the brunt of the man's displeasure bravely.

"Help me out here, girls," she said. "I think Clint is about to blow his top."

"Oh, don't you worry," said Tina. "We've got your back."

"Yeah, us girls have to stick together," said Joanna.

Only Jackie wasn't in a solidarity frame of mind. "What did you do?" she asked.

But then Clint was upon them, and he was looking like a steam engine about to explode.

"You're a cop!" he screamed accusingly. "You're a damn cop!"

"No, I'm not a cop," said Odelia calmly as she came face to face with the women snatcher. "But my uncle is, and he'll be very interested to know what kind of operation you're running here, Mr. Bunda."

"Oh, so now suddenly it's Mr. Bunda, huh?" He grabbed Odelia's arm. "Come. All of you. You, too, Kimmy."

"Yes, sir," said Kimmy quietly.

"I'm not going anywhere with you," said Odelia defensively as she yanked her arm free from the man's grasp.

"I've got them all lined up and we're going to get to the bottom of this thing once and for all," said Clint.

"Lined up who?" asked Tina.

"All of my people, who do you think? One of them must be involved in this thing, and I wanna know who. I wanna know who'd betray me like this!" he screamed, raising his fists to the sky and shaking them violently.

The man was losing it, Odelia thought, and she was starting to get a little scared.

But Clint was already heading back to the main villa, and Kimmy was shrugging her shoulders. She clearly didn't see a way out either.

"Where's the boat?" asked Odelia. "There's got to be a boat we can take to get off the island."

"It's not what you think it is, Odelia," said Kimmy, quite surprisingly. "Your uncle called Clint just now, telling him the whole story."

"What?!" Odelia cried.

"Yeah, I was hiding under the bed, and I heard the whole thing. Alec even told him about my involvement. He says he's found the women."

"My uncle has found them?"

"Apparently the FBI got wind of the affair and got in touch with Alec, and together they managed to convince the families that something very bad was going on. They finally managed to track down all five women. They're safe now."

"But… Clint?"

"Clint's got nothing to do with it. But someone on the team does. And he's going to try and figure out who it is."

Odelia glanced down at her cats, who both shrugged. "Okay," she finally said, and joined Kimmy and the other three women in pursuit of Clint, whom they could hear screaming all the way to the jacuzzi as he made his way back to the main house.

"What's all this about kidnapped women?" asked Joanna.

"I'll explain later," said Odelia.

"You're a cop?" asked Jackie, sounding distinctly unhappy.

"No, I'm a reporter."

"I asked Odelia to come and look into a possible kidnapping ring centered around Passion Island," Kimmy explained, drawing gasps of shock from the other three women.

But by then they'd arrived at the villa, where Clint was pacing in front of his collected staff, all gathered in front of the main house.

"Someone here has been working against me!" he announced. "One of you has decided to use my show—MY SHOW—for nefarious purposes! And I want you to step forward right now and reveal yourself!"

Odelia had crossed her arms in front of her and stood watching the scene with some trepidation. She didn't know what to think. She'd figured Clint was the man behind the kidnapping ring, but apparently her uncle didn't think he was, and Uncle Alec was a smart cookie, so he probably had his reasons.

"No one?" asked Clint. "All right. So be it." He picked his phone from his pocket and quickly dialed a number.

"What's happening?" asked Tina, as bewildered as the rest of the small crowd that had gathered in the rising sun.

"No idea," said Odelia truthfully.

"Alec? Yeah, nobody's talking. So you do as we arranged. Yeah, you place that call now." He disconnected, then let his gaze rake across the faces of his people, none too friendly. If looks could kill, they'd all have fallen to the ground, dead.

Suddenly, a ringtone pierced the silence—it was the sound of birdsong.

"You're busted!" Clint bellowed. "Busted!"

Everyone looked around with consternation written all over their features, as Clint dove into the crowd, which parted like the Red Sea before Moses. And there, on the ground, was a phone, buzzing away, still blasting out a steady whoop-whoop-whoop.

Clint picked it up. "Who does this phone belong to! Who, dammit!"

Eyes swiveled, and heads turned left and right, but whoever the phone belonged to didn't make themselves known, causing Clint to stomp the ground like a petulant child. "Reveal yourself!" he demanded heatedly.

"It belongs to Rick," said Max. "I'd recognize that ringtone anywhere."

"It belongs to Rick," Odelia echoed.

"Oh, crap," the pale techie muttered, and suddenly broke into an awkward run!

"Stop!" Clint screamed. "Stop that man!"

But since everyone was gathered around him, there was

no one left to stop Rick, as the skinny techie disappeared around the bend.

"After him!" Clint ordered. "Whoever catches that bastard gets a fat bonus!"

As one man, all of those gathered now moved off in a minor stampede, all in pursuit of the man named Rick, whom Odelia had recognized as the guy who'd installed a camera right above her bed.

She joined the runners, as did everyone else. No one wanted to miss the grand finale to this very strange and unexpected drama. Even the cameramen, who'd dutifully filmed the entire scene, broke into a jog, and kept right on filming.

They finally arrived at a small dock, where a boat was moored. Rick, who had secured himself a nice head start, was already climbing aboard, and throwing off the moorings.

"He's getting away!" Clint cried. "Stop him!"

But it was obvious they'd never get there in time. As they neared, Rick was pushing the boat away from the dock, and had started up the engine. He was going to make a clean getaway while they all watched.

And he was waving at them, looking pretty triumphant, when suddenly a second boat appeared out of nowhere. And as Rick was looking in their direction he never noticed the other boat sailing alongside and a tall, lanky figure leaping from boat to boat, like a regular Jack Sparrow, though minus the funky eyeliner.

"It's Chase!" Odelia cried happily, and she now saw two more familiar figures on this second boat: Gran and Scarlett!

"Gotcha!" Clint yelled, shaking his fist. "Well done, son! Well done!"

Chase had managed to capture the errant technician, and was now steering the boat back to the dock, leaving the other boat drifting aimlessly, and Gran and Scarlett looking a little ill at ease at the prospect of soon becoming prey to the Gulf of Thailand's relentless currents and ending up in the Philippines.

But before long, several people had jumped into the water, and were making their way over to assist Chase in subduing Rick, while others swam over to the second boat and managed to bring it to the dock in next to no time, no doubt earning them a debt of gratitude, and a kiss from Scarlett, the oldest seductress in Passion Island's history.

"Why!" cried Clint as soon as Rick had been brought safely to shore. "Why did you do it!"

Rick shrugged, and didn't look entirely happy, faced with a minor mob and several cameras pointed at his pockmarked face. "For the money, what do you think?"

"So you're behind this kidnapping business?" asked Chase.

"I'm just a minor cog in a big wheel," said Rick. "I'm the guy who sends the footage, and arranges for the personal information of the candidates to be sent to the potential buyers."

"Potential buyers?" asked Clint, making a powerful effort not to smack the man in the face.

"Yeah, you'd be surprised how many people out there are willing to pay through the nose for the privilege of acquiring one of Passion Island's contestants," said Rick. "I'm talking millions."

"People are buying Passion Island contestants?" asked Tina, shocked.

"Yeah, five of them," said Chase.

"They've all been found," Clint assured them. "And I swear I didn't have a clue."

"You could have taken the reports that those women were

missing a little more seriously, though," said Kimmy accusingly.

Clint, perhaps for the first time in his life, contrived to look moderately contrite. "Yeah, I probably should have done that little thing," he confessed.

"Instead you wanted to keep the show running, and didn't care one hoot that you were putting people in danger," Kimmy continued.

"I didn't know, okay!"

"So who are these buyers?" asked Odelia.

Rick shrugged. "Russian oligarchs, Arabian billionaires, Chinese mobsters... Passion Island isn't just wildly popular with your regular audience, but with the criminal element, too, and those with enough money to burn decided they wanted a piece of the action—literally—and so a couple of very enterprising people set up a business to give them what they wanted."

"This is sick," said Joanna, looking nauseous.

"Don't worry, sweetheart," said Clint. "They only targeted blondes. Like Odelia."

Chase then strode forward and gave the producer a single punch to the face. It was enough to land the man on the sandy ground, wondering who'd turned off the lights.

Loud cheers and applause broke out amongst Clint's staff.

Apparently the man wasn't as popular as he thought—nor as free of responsibility in the drama that had just unfolded.

Next to Odelia, Tina heaved a little sigh. "I guess this is the end of Passion Island."

"I think so," Odelia admitted.

Tina broke into a smile. "Good. I was fed up with being stalked by seducers anyway."

Chase walked up to Odelia, and grabbed her into his arms for a bone-crushing hug.

"I missed you, babe," he breathed passionately.

"And I missed you," she said.

And then they kissed, and more applause broke out.

They might not have won that fifty grand, but they had caught their guy.

EPILOGUE

"I've never been contacted by the FBI before," said Uncle Alec, sounding particularly proud of the fact. "So when they told me they'd freed the women and arrested the bad guys, all I needed to do was call Clint Bunda and get him to play ball. The feds had the number of the kidnappers' contact on the island but didn't have a name, so I placed the call, and the rest is history." Next to him, Charlene Butterwick was beaming, clearly proud of her man, as evidenced by the fact that she kept patting his hand.

"You did a wonderful thing, Alec," said Hampton Cove's mayor. "A wonderful, wonderful thing."

"Oh, I don't know about that," said Uncle Alec, modestly plucking an imaginary piece of lint from his polo shirt. "Some people call me a hero, others call me a savior. I just like to think I did my duty, same as anyone would."

We were finally home again, after a long journey, and not a moment too soon. Traveling by plane and car, I was happy to be back, and so were my friends.

Harriet and Brutus, who'd risked life and limb by traveling on that boat with Chase and Gran and Scarlett, had had the scare of a lifetime when Chase had steered the vessel straight into Rick's boat. For a moment, Harriet had told me, she'd feared the boat would be lost with all hands—and paws. Luckily that hadn't happened, but she'd been happy to feel terra firma under her shaky paws, that's for sure.

As for Rick, he'd been collected by the police and locked up with the rest of the human traffickers. The women had been freed from the clutches of the rich men who'd had them snatched for their own personal enjoyment, and justice had finally prevailed.

As far as Passion Island was concerned, the network had decided to take the show off the air, as well as every other reality show like it. Lawyers would presumably have a field day working out culpability, as the families of all five women had decided to sue.

"It's a pity that they canceled the show, though," said Gran, offering the contrarian view as usual. "I think it had potential. Especially with Scarlett and myself on board."

"Yeah, I think we could have taken that show to the next level," Scarlett agreed, as she subjected the sausage Tex had deposited on her plate with a touch of suspicion. Like the proverbial pit, it was black from pole to pole, and didn't look fit for human consumption.

Tex and Marge had returned from their trip the moment they heard what danger their daughter had escaped from. They'd missed a big chunk of their European vacation, but had vowed to make up for it next year, turning this travel bug into a regular thing.

"If I'd known how much trouble you were putting yourself in I'd never have allowed you to go through with it," Marge said censoriously, clucking like a worried mother hen. "Promise me you'll never put yourself in danger like that again, Odelia. Promise me now."

"I promise," said Odelia, but I could see she was crossing her fingers behind her back.

"What is she doing, Max?" asked Dooley, gesturing to the strange custom.

"She's lying to her mother," said Harriet. "Making promises she won't keep."

"You mean she'd go through the Passion Island ordeal again?" asked Dooley, surprised. "Willingly?"

"Yeah, I guess so," said Brutus. "Let's face it, though. She was never in any danger."

We'd all heard the reports of the unmarked vans snatching the five other women off the street, their takers setting up an elaborate ruse to make the families believe they were all right—four to get married to the men of their dreams, the fifth on a spiritual kick. What had tipped off the FBI was that one of the women had managed to escape, and had started a chain of reactions leading to the arrest of Rick on Passion Island.

Tex, working relentlessly at the grill, was happily flipping burgers like a pro again, providing his family sustenance. If anything, though, his very particular set of skills was getting worse, which seemed impossible. Usually humans get better with practice, but not our good doctor Poole. Still, he was clearly having a ball, and that's all that matters.

"So when is the show coming out?" asked Scarlett now. "I can't wait to see myself in action." She preened a little as she spoke the words.

"The show isn't coming out, sweetheart," said Gran. "The show has been canceled. As in buried deep within the archives of the network, never to be seen again, except maybe by wizened old scholars working on a dissertation on reality show history."

"But… what about all that footage?"

"Buried. Deep," said Gran. "Like Indiana Jones's Ark of the Covenant."

"So I worked my seductive ass off for nothing?!" cried Scarlett, visibly upset.

"The joy is not in reaching your destination, but in the journey," said Charlene, earning herself a scathing look from Scarlett and wisely shutting up. A good politician knows when to speak, but also knows when to be quiet.

"I'm glad Odelia wasn't kidnapped," said Dooley. "I don't think she would have liked to spend time with a Russian oligarch, an Arabian billionaire or a Chinese mobster. And I don't think we would have liked it either."

"They wouldn't have kidnapped us, Dooley," Harriet said. "They would have snatched Odelia, not her cats."

"But... they'd have simply left us behind?" He looked shocked at the prospect.

"These people aren't exactly cat lovers, Dooley," said Brutus. "Probably they like dogs, though. Big, mean, tough canines. Not sweet pussies like you and me."

"Or me," said Harriet.

"Or me," I said, nodding.

Dooley shivered visibly. "Imagine. Having to spend time with a mean dog when you're a cat person like Odelia. The horror."

I shared a look with Brutus and Harriet, and we were in silent agreement that we weren't going to tell Dooley that when being kidnapped by a human trafficker to be traded to a rich pervert having to spend time with dogs probably wasn't the worst part.

Instead, I snapped a piece of steak out of the air that Odelia threw me. She'd already cut off the burnt parts, and had saved only the succulent center. I nodded my thanks and gulped the whole thing down eagerly.

For a moment, only the sound of chewing filled the air, as

four cats devoured their portions. Then, Harriet said, "You know? Being on Passion Island has really made me think."

"Oh?" I said, swallowing with relish.

She gave me a sweet smile. "I missed you guys. I mean, I know we don't always get along. And I know I can be something of a pain in the patootie sometimes—"

"Oh, no," I began to say, but she stopped me with a gesture of her paw.

"No, it's true, Max. But deep down you know that I love you guys, right?"

I nodded, swallowing again, only this time it wasn't a tasty morsel of meat but a lump in my throat.

"I love you guys, too," said Brutus a little gruffly. "And if you tell anyone, I'll kill you."

"I love you guys so much!" said Dooley, sniffling unabashedly.

And thus ended our Thai adventure. And as a mild summer rain suddenly started falling from the sky, instigating a mad dash for the great indoors from all those present, and a mad scramble from Tex to safeguard his grill, I smiled. After the sweltering heat of the Thai isles, and the hair-raising antics of Passion Island producers, a light drizzle was just what we all needed.

And when I jumped off the porch swing and padded into the backyard, to sample some of that soft rain on my skin, I was accompanied by my three friends. The scent of summer and fresh grass tickled my sense of smell, and I whooped with joy. The humans, all ensconced on the porch now, probably thought we were crazy, but for once we defied the old adage that cats hate to get wet.

I was getting soaked and I loved it.

Home sweet home!

ABOUT NIC

Nic Saint is the pen name for writing couple Nick and Nicole Saint. They've penned novels in the romance, cat sleuth, middle grade, suspense, comedy and cozy mystery genres. Nicole has a background in accounting and Nick in political science and before being struck by the writing bug the Saints worked odd jobs around the world (including massage therapist in Mexico, gardener in Italy, restaurant manager in India, and Berlitz teacher in Belgium).

When they're not writing they enjoy Christmas-themed Hallmark movies (whether it's Christmas or not), all manner of pastry, comic books, a daily dose of yoga (to limber up those limbs), and spoiling their big red tomcat Tommy.

www.nicsaint.com

The Mysteries of Max

Purrfect Murder ~ *9*

Purrfectly Deadly *2*

Purrfect Revenge — *3*

Purrfect Heat ~ *4*

Purrfect Crime — *5*

Purrfect Rivalry — *6*

Purrfect Peril — *7*

Purrfect Secret — *8*

Purrfect Alibi — *9*

Purrfect Obsession — *10*

Purrfect Betrayal — *11*

Purrfectly Clueless — *12*

Purrfectly Royal — *13*

Purrfect Cut — *14*

Purrfect Trap — *15*

Purrfectly Hidden — *16*

Purrfect Kill — *17*

Purrfect Boy Toy — *18*

Purrfectly Dogged — *19*

Purrfectly Dead — *20*

Purrfect Saint — *21*

Purrfect Advice — *22*

Purrfect Passion — *23*

Box Set 1 (Books 1-3)

Box Set 2 (Books 4-6)

Box Set 3 (Books 7-9)

Box Set 4 (Books 10-12)

Box Set 5 (Books 13-15)

Box Set 6 (Books 16-18)

Box Set 7 (Books 19-21)

Purrfect Santa

Purrfectly Flealess

Nora Steel

Murder Retreat

The Kellys

Murder Motel

Death in Suburbia

Emily Stone

Murder at the Art Class

Washington & Jefferson

First Shot

Alice Whitehouse

Spooky Times

Spooky Trills

Spooky End

Spooky Spells

Ghosts of London

Between a Ghost and a Spooky Place

Public Ghost Number One

Ghost Save the Queen

Box Set 1 (Books 1-3)

A Tale of Two Harrys

Ghost of Girlband Past

Ghostlier Things

Charleneland

Deadly Ride

Final Ride

Neighborhood Witch Committee

Witchy Start

Witchy Worries

Witchy Wishes

Saffron Diffley

Crime and Retribution

Vice and Verdict

Felonies and Penalties (Saffron Diffley Short 1)

The B-Team

Once Upon a Spy

Tate-à-Tate

Enemy of the Tates

Ghosts vs. Spies

The Ghost Who Came in from the Cold

Witchy Fingers

Witchy Trouble

Witchy Hexations

Witchy Possessions

Witchy Riches

Box Set 1 (Books 1-4)

The Mysteries of Bell & Whitehouse

One Spoonful of Trouble

Two Scoops of Murder

Three Shots of Disaster

Box Set 1 (Books 1-3)

A Twist of Wraith

A Touch of Ghost

A Clash of Spooks

Box Set 2 (Books 4-6)

The Stuffing of Nightmares

A Breath of Dead Air

An Act of Hodd

Box Set 3 (Books 7-9)

A Game of Dons

Standalone Novels

When in Bruges

The Whiskered Spy

ThrillFix

Homejacking

The Eighth Billionaire

The Wrong Woman

Printed in Great Britain
by Amazon

50598182R00118